OMAR RISING

Also by Aisha Saeed

Amal Unbound
Written in the Stars

OMAR RISING

Aisha Saeed

 Nancy Paulsen Books

NANCY PAULSEN BOOKS

An imprint of Penguin Random House LLC, New York

First published in the United States of America by Nancy Paulsen Books,
an imprint of Penguin Random House LLC, 2022

Visit us online at penguinrandomhouse.com

Library of Congress Cataloging-in-Publication Data
Names: Saeed, Aisha, author.
Title: Omar rising / Aisha Saeed.
Description: New York: Nancy Paulsen Books, [2022]
Summary: Seventh-grader Omar must contend with being treated like a second-class
citizen when he gets a scholarship to an elite boarding school in Pakistan.
Identifiers: LCCN 2021032381 | ISBN 9780593108581 (hardcover)
ISBN 9780593108598 (ebook)
Subjects: CYAC: Boarding schools—Fiction. | Schools—Fiction. | Pakistan—Fiction.
Classification: LCC PZ7.L4425 Ran 2003 | DDC [Fic]—dc23
LC record available at https://lccn.loc.gov/2021032381

Book manufactured in Canada
ISBN 9780593108581
1 3 5 7 9 10 8 6 4 2

FRI

Design by Nicole Rheingans
Text set in Stone Seri ITC Std.

For every Omar out there—never stop believing in yourself.

Chapter 1

August of wind blows through the field as my friends and I wrap up our soccer game. It rustles through the neat rows of sugarcane growing behind us and sweeps over the orange trees in the distance.

"That does it!" Fuad shouts. He kicks the soccer ball toward me. "I'm never playing with either of you again. I mean it this time."

"Don't be such a sore loser," Zaki responds. "It was a fun game."

"Only because you and Omar cheated," Fuad says, pointing at me.

I tilt my head. "Why is it whenever you win, it's a hard-earned victory, but if anyone else does, they're cheating?"

"Admit it," Zaki says. "Omar's last goal was epic."

"Fine," Fuad says grudgingly. "It wasn't that bad."

"I'll take it." I grin. Coming from Fuad, halfhearted praise is basically a standing ovation.

The soccer ball rolls until it settles next to my foot. As I kick it up to prop it under my arm, a wave of sadness washes over me. Fuad always vows never to play with us again, but this really *is* the last time I'll be kicking the ball with him. There have been so many lasts lately. My last walk to the market yesterday. My last time feeding the chickens this morning. And tonight will be my last night sleeping in my own bed.

Tomorrow, everything will change. Tomorrow, I head to boarding school: the Ghalib Academy for Boys. Which means very soon my home, my village, and scrimmage games like these will no longer be part of my ordinary, everyday life.

It's not that I don't want to go. I filled out the forms myself. Asked my teacher for a recommendation. Sorted vegetables at the produce stand and cut sugarcane in the fields to save up for the application fee.

When I got the call, my mother's eyes lit up like a thousand stars. She hugged me so tight I thought she'd never let go. The son of a servant getting a scholarship to a place like Ghalib? It would open up my world in ways

I could only begin to imagine. Now better things are actually within reach, like college and a job that earns enough money to buy a home for my mother and me. A *real* home, with bedrooms and sofas and rugs, not a one-room space where we've strung up curtains that we pretend are walls. Ghalib is a once-in-a-lifetime opportunity to rewrite my destiny.

"Isn't that Amal?" Zaki asks. He points toward the gravel road that slices through our village.

Following his gaze, I brighten. Fuad and Zaki are good friends, but Amal is like family. My mother works for her parents, and we live on their property, behind their house. Born three days apart, we've never known life without each other.

"Your mother asked me to find you," Amal says when she approaches with two of her younger sisters in tow. "She said it was important."

"Time for your partyyy!" Amal's three-year-old sister sings out.

"Safa!" Amal grimaces.

"But don't say anything," says four-year-old Rabia, placing a finger solemnly on her lips. "It's a surprise!"

"It's okay." I laugh, looking at Amal's stricken expression. "Fozia Auntie asked me for a list of my favorite sweets the other day. And Fuad let it slip when we started playing."

"No one around here can keep a secret except me, huh?" Amal exclaims.

"Nope. Never." I shake my head.

"Everyone's just excited for you," says Zaki.

"Tell me about it." Fuad rolls his eyes. "My dad won't stop going on and on. 'Why can't you be more like Omar? You need to apply yourself.' If I didn't like you so much, I'd probably hate you."

"I just got lucky." I flush.

"There's no lucky about it," Amal says. "You earned it fair and square. Tomorrow will be amazing."

"Tomorrow?" Zaki repeats. "But school doesn't start till next week."

"Ghalib starts a week earlier," I remind him.

"So today really *was* the last soccer game?" Fuad's expression falls.

"It's not like I'm moving to Jupiter," I say. "I'll be back. Winter break. Summer—"

"Yeah," Fuad interrupts. "But it won't be . . ." His voice trails off.

But I know what he was going to say. And he's right. It won't be the same. Not even close.

"So, are you ready for the *partyyy*?" Amal teases as the six of us walk down the road toward her home.

"I tried *all* the sweets," Safa says.

"The laddu was my favorite!" Rabia chimes in.

"Thanks for the taste-testing," I tell them.

When we reach the front door, Amal looks at me. "Pretend to be surprised, okay? Please? Everyone's so excited."

"I'll do my very best," I promise.

But it isn't hard to look surprised. As soon as Amal opens the door, my jaw drops. Her home is packed! Neighbors fill the main room and spill into the courtyard outside. Fairy lights are strung along the windows.

"There's the man of the hour!" Fozia Auntie sings out. She stands beside a table covered with trays and trays of sweets.

Everyone claps and cheers.

"Wow." I blink. "Thank you!"

"Great work, Omar." Amal's mother ruffles my hair.

"Always knew you could do it," says another neighbor.

"That's right." Fozia Auntie nods. "It's not every day someone from our village heads off to one of the most prestigious schools in Pakistan."

"More like not *ever*," her daughter Hafsa chimes in. "You're the first to get into a school like that, but you won't be the last!" The crowd laughs.

"Oh." I shift. "I don't—"

"It's true." Amal's father, Malik Uncle, smiles. "You carry all of our pride with you, Omar. Carry it well."

Looking at everyone's beaming faces, I'm filled with a warm glow. I thank my neighbors, then grab a plate and fill it with carroty gajrela, yellow laddus, and sticky-sweet jalebis. So many desserts I can't fit them all on my plate—I'll have to come back for seconds, maybe thirds! My friends and I settle at the edge of the open-air courtyard as Banu and Shamu, the two farm kittens, beeline straight for me. Shamu sidles up to me and purrs. Banu sniffs the sweets on my plate.

"Sorry," I say. They know I'm usually reliable for sneaking them leftovers. "Pretty sure cats can't have jalebis."

Fuad picks up a round laddu. "All right. Who can catch this in their mouth?"

"What do I get if I do?" Zaki counters.

"Ultimate respect?" I suggest.

Fuad leans back and torpedoes the sweet at Zaki. It bounces against his nose before landing in his lap. We burst out laughing.

I glance at Amal refilling trays. The kittens at my feet. These people. This place. It's all I've ever known. Soon, it will become a memory.

I know I'm leaving to make a new life—a better one—but I hate how beginnings have to be tied to endings. That in order to start the next part of my journey, I'll have to leave all I know behind.

Chapter 2

What a nice party," my mother says the next day. She sits on a stool by our partly opened front door, mending an old sweater. "You did a good job pretending to be surprised."

"Wait!" My eyes widen. "How'd you know I knew?"

"Nothing stays secret in this village." She chuckles. "Least of all a party. Although I never let it slip, and you and I *live* together!"

I glance at my mother. *This* is the part I've tried not to think about. It's been the two of us as long as I can remember. My father died soon after I was born. Once I leave, she'll be alone.

Amal pokes her head around the door. "All packed?"

"I think so," I tell her. "But I keep feeling like I'm forgetting something."

"It's okay if you do. My dad can always drop it off. The school isn't that far away."

"It's far enough."

"Only twenty kilometers," my mother chimes in.

"May as well be two hundred. It's too far to get home much. I won't be back until winter break."

"Probably for the best," my mother says. "You're there to focus on your studies. Not everyone gets this kind of opportunity."

"People are desperate to get in," Amal adds. "I'm thinking of applying to the girls' school next fall. Hafsa's working on her application now."

"Iqra?" I look at her. "That's great! Of course you should!"

"I'm only *thinking* about it," Amal says quickly. "There's a lot that needs to happen first, like seeing if I even get in and figuring out how we'd pay for it. It's expensive."

"Well, I think living inside a school would be the ultimate dream for you."

"Very funny, Omar."

"Who's joking?" I grin. "And don't get me wrong, I'm excited about Ghalib . . . I am."

"You should be! And if you need us, we'll be only a phone call away," Amal says.

My stomach unclenches a bit. This is true. Amal always knows the exact right thing to say to help me feel better.

"I'll call every day," I promise.

"Uh, every day?" She laughs. "I don't think so. Between school, soccer, chess club, and whatever, you're not going to have time to think of us, much less call."

"Mr. Adeel said at orientation that the astronomy club is exploring exoplanets this year. I'm definitely joining that."

"And soccer, for sure," Amal says.

"Don't know if I'll make the cut. They won the regional championship last year."

"But you're so good!" Amal says. "How about archery? And robotics. I'd sign up for those if I were you."

"Maybe all of the above?" I grin.

"Now, wait a second," my mother interrupts. "You two sound like Safa in a candy shop."

"It's just exciting to have so many choices! But you know what *I'm* most jealous about?" Amal asks.

"Hmmm, I wonder. The library, maybe?"

"Don't joke! You're so lucky, Omar. I hear Ghalib's library is enormous. Let's pick a title and do a book club when you're back for winter break."

"Amal—"

"I'll even let you pick a book on outer space or science fiction . . ."

"Amal, listen. I think our book-club days are over for a while," I tell her. "I doubt I'll have time to read for fun. Classes are supposed to be really hard."

"You can try. If I could find time to read while catching up on an entire semester of school, you can squeeze a book or two in."

I bite my lip. She's right about that. Amal went through a terrible time this past year and had to drop out of school. Life only recently returned to normal for her, and she had to work so hard to catch up. The last person who needs to hear any complaints from me is her.

"Oh! I almost forgot." I reach into my pocket and pull out a necklace. It's a thin loop with a sparrow pendant. I saved up to buy it for Amal last month, but Safa immediately broke the clasp.

"You fixed it!" Amal exclaims.

"It wasn't too hard. Your father lent me pliers, and I bent the broken bit back in place. The tough part will be making sure Safa doesn't get her hands on it again."

She looks down at the sparrow and then at me. Her expression grows clouded.

"I'm going to miss you," she says.

"I'll miss you, too." I swallow.

"What's with the long faces?" my mother asks. She stands and drapes an arm around each of us. "This is a new adventure. It's what all of us have been hoping for."

There's a knock on our door. And then—

"Omar?" Malik Uncle peeks in. "I'm ready when you are."

I pick up my suitcase and step into the yard. The hot August sun beats against my skin. This same sun will be there to warm me at Ghalib, too.

Uncle's motorcycle idles in the distance. My mother pulls me to her and hugs me. When we part, tears fill her eyes.

"I'm proud of you, Omar," she says. "I can't wait to see all you will do."

"For us," I tell her.

"For us."

Chapter 3

I've always known what I want to be when I grow up. In fifth year, I read the classroom copy of *Our Galaxy* so many times, my teacher got the next book in the series, *Beyond the Milky Way*, just for me. There are over four thousand known planets orbiting outside our solar system, and scientists find new ones each year. That's what I want to do. Discover planets. Maybe even entire galaxies. But right now, as Malik Uncle's motorcycle speeds over potholes, I hang on and hope he doesn't personally launch us into another solar system.

Arriving at Ghalib Academy's parking lot, I take in the shiny sedans of all shapes, colors, and sizes. I've never seen so many cars in one place. Back home, most of us get around on foot or motorcycles or take rickshaws. But there's no brightly colored rickshaw in sight, and our motorcycle is the only one here.

Kids hurry across the lawn toward a tent that says *Student Registration*, their mothers and fathers not far behind. My chest tightens. Everyone here is with their parents. Am I the only one who's not?

"Registration line's filling up." Uncle unties my suitcase from the rear. He gestures to the tent. "Shall we?"

I hesitate. One of his workers quit a few days ago, and orange-planting season is fast approaching. He took time out of his day to even bring me here. But before I can say any of this, he speaks again.

"This is a big day," he says. "Your mother will want all the details."

"That's true." I crack a smile. "Thanks."

Butterflies dance in my stomach as we near the tent where kids laugh and high-five each other. In the distance I see Marwan and Jibril—two other seventh years I met at orientation—but otherwise, it's a sea of strangers.

"Name?" a lady with red-framed glasses asks when it's my turn.

"Omar Ali."

"There we are. First name in the pile." She hands me a folder with *SB* stamped on the front.

"What does this mean?" I point to the letters.

"Oh, that? Don't worry." She waves a hand. "They'll explain at assembly next week."

I wasn't worried until she told me *not* to worry. I want to ask her more, but Uncle taps my shoulder. "Let's see your room before I have to leave."

"The rooms aren't too exciting," I warn. "They pack so much into them, you can touch one bed with your foot while sitting on the other."

"In that case, let's hope you have a good roommate."

I hope so, too. Having a roommate—a total stranger I'll share a room with for a year—is the weirdest part about all this. I run my hand over the pouch in my book bag where I stored a baggie of guava-flavored candy. My summer roommate was great—Kareem, a scholarship kid like me. Tall, lanky, and full of jokes, he always kept a stash of candy on him and was quick to share it. I hoped bringing some would be a good icebreaker, but mostly I'm just hoping I'll get a roommate as nice as him again.

I lead Uncle across the main campus to where the dorms are situated. But when I punch in the three-digit code from summer, the door doesn't budge.

"I got it!" A boy hurries over to us. He's taller than me by a foot, and his floppy black hair is draped over his forehead.

"It's one-three-five." He punches in the code. "They change it every month. Didn't you get the email?"

"Oh. I don't have an account set up yet."

"No big deal." He smiles. "If you didn't register at home, you can get it set up at the computer lab. There's information on all that in your folder."

Emails. People here have probably used email since they were babies. Another thing to add to the list of stuff I'll need to figure out quickly.

"I'm Faisal. If you have questions, I'm in the upperclassmen dorms. See you!"

"Kids here seem nice," Uncle says as we step inside. I check my sheet: 2-2. My room is the second one on the second floor.

We enter, and the space is set up just like the room I had for summer orientation. Two twin beds with nightstands on opposite walls. Next to each, a wooden dresser, a desk, and chair.

"This is a *fantastic* setup!" Uncle exclaims. "One of my cousins went to a boarding school, and there were six boys to a room there." He glances around and then at me. "It's really happening, isn't it? You did it, Omar."

"I can't believe it."

"Believe it." His eyes crinkle with a smile. "May the pride

we all feel in you lift you up and help you succeed. Ameen."

I bite my lip. I know everyone rooting for me is a good thing. But right now the weight of that responsibility sinks in me like stones.

Uncle hugs me goodbye. I watch him disappear down the stairs. And then he's gone. Back to our village. Back home.

"Hey, Omar, looks like we're neighbors!" a voice from across the hallway calls out. I recognize Humza from the summer. "I brought the Mohamed Salah jersey I told you about. Wanna check it out?"

"I'll be there in a second," I tell him.

I rest my suitcase on my bed and look out the window. The soccer field is right below my window, and some kids are already playing. At the edge of the field there's a wall with a mural teeming with students doing all sorts of cool stuff, like playing instruments, shooting hoops, scoring goals, and even doing science experiments. Bunsen burners are fired up and beakers ooze with smoky liquids. Straight across from me, the figure of a boy peers through a telescope up at the sky.

I squeeze the windowsill until my fingers grow white. I'm only twenty kilometers from home, but I'm in a whole different orbit. Still, there is no room for homesickness or regret. For the next few years, Planet Ghalib is home.

Chapter 4

Hey, roomie," a voice calls out, and Kareem saunters into the room holding a worn duffel bag.

"No way!" I brighten. "We're roommates again?"

"Looks that way." He gives me a fist bump. "I was worried it'd be Naveed."

"Naveed?" I raise my eyebrows. "He's great!"

"Don't get me wrong! Love the guy. But remember how he snored? We could hear him down the hallway."

"True." I laugh. "His roommate slept with headphones on."

"I sleep as light as a cat, so that would've been awful."

"Where are your parents?"

"They didn't need to walk me up. My duffel bag was pretty light."

He shrugs like it doesn't matter. But I get it. Kareem's a scholarship kid like me. His parents probably didn't have time to linger. He sticks his duffel bag on his desk.

"Brought something for you," I say. I grab the bag of candy and toss it to him.

"Guava!" He sits down on his bed and pops one in his mouth. He closes his eyes. "Mmm. I thought no one could beat Danawala's stall back home, but *this* is good candy."

"Next time I'll get you the lychee-flavored ones. Those are pretty yummy, too."

"Thanks, Omar! I owe you."

"Repay me with a soccer scrimmage once we're unpacked? We have a great view of the field from here."

"Thinking of trying out for the team?" He cranes his neck to look out the window.

"I'm not sure," I say. "But yeah, maybe. I'm definitely joining the astronomy club. What about you?"

"Debate club for sure," he says. "Made it to semifinals at my last school. Think I'll try out for basketball, too."

"Maybe after we kick the soccer ball around, you can show me how to play basketball?"

"You'll be learning from the best!"

There's a knock at the door. It's Naveed.

"The gang is officially back," Kareem exclaims. He gives Naveed a fist bump. We join him in the hallway.

"I'm so glad we're on the same floor again!" Naveed pushes his glasses up the bridge of his nose. "Remember Jibril? He's my roommate. I can't figure out if he's nice or not. If he's mean, can I squeeze in with both of you?"

"Jibril? He's great, and besides, who'd be mean to *you*?" I playfully swat his arm. "Listen, we're going to play soccer once we finish unpacking. I saw some—"

"Move over." A gruff voice interrupts us. It's a man in a three-piece suit accompanied by two servants in plain shalwar kamiz carrying enormous suitcases.

We step aside as they brush past us into the room next door. A boy with short spiky hair emerges from the staircase. His eyes are locked on the screen of his fancy silver phone.

Naveed looks at the boy and then back at us. "Okay . . . well . . . see you all later." He darts down the hallway.

Before Kareem or I can move, an angry voice—the man's—ricochets against the cinder-block walls next door.

"They must be joking! How can anyone live in a room like this?" he barks. "I'm not paying for a new gym so Aiden can live in a prison cell, am I?"

A prison cell? Kareem and I exchange glances.

Moments later, he storms past us. The hallway vibrates from his angry departure.

"Nice guy," I say under my breath.

The boy looks up from his phone. His eyes meet mine.

"What?" He frowns.

"Oh," I begin. "Nothing. I just . . . Hi. My name's Omar, and this is—"

But before I can finish my sentence, he stalks into his room, slamming the door shut behind him.

"He's a friendly one," I say to Kareem as we retreat into our room.

"Must take after his dad."

I laugh, and we get to work organizing our things. I unpack my clothes and set a photo of my mother and me on the nightstand. I tack up my poster of the Milky Way. Kareem's taping up a photo of cricket legend Wasim Akram by his bed. In a few minutes, our room looks a little less stark and a little more like us.

Glancing into the hallway, I see Aiden's servants still waiting around. The older one leans against the cinderblock wall, his eyes half-closed.

I grab my chair and drag it toward the door. "Would you like to sit? We have another you could also borrow."

The older man eyes the chair and hesitates. "Thank you, but we're fine standing," he finally says.

I can tell that's not true by how uncomfortable he looks. He's old enough to be my grandfather. I'm glad my mother was never treated this way. Amal's family feels like our own. But I know this is the lot of many servants—expected to stand at command while awaiting the next order from their employer. It's the fate I'm here to avoid.

"Please, chota sahib." The other man puts his palms up. "We're happy to stand. Really."

I wince at the term *little sir*. They don't know I'm more like them than most people here.

When Aiden's father returns, we edge closer to our open door.

"Well, they can say goodbye to the rest of the gymnasium money," he says.

"So, we're leaving?" Aiden asks.

"For now, you'll stay."

"But you said if they couldn't change my room, we'd go!"

"I know what I said, but—"

"You're really going to make me stay? In this dump?"

Dump? Kareem mouths silently.

"I thought it was a prison," I whisper.

Kareem flops backward onto his bed and laughs.

"You *could* have been at Aitchison." The man's voice grows harder. "If your grades had been better, I wouldn't be sending you here in the first place. How about instead of complaining, get your marks where they need to be. In the meantime, be grateful I got you a single."

"That man acts like he owns the place," I whisper.

"Sounds like he does own the gym. Aiden should move in there. It's definitely bigger than the dorms."

"Plus, all the basketball you can play."

"Now, *that's* the dream." Kareem grins.

After they leave, Aiden's door slams with such a shuddering force, the wall between us trembles. Loud music fills the air. Angry. Pulsing. The floor beneath us vibrates.

"I'd take Naveed's snoring over this." Kareem grimaces.

"He'll cool off soon," I say.

"We were going to play soccer anyway," Kareem says. "Let's join those kids out back."

I side-eye Aiden's closed door as we leave. Maybe the room is small to him, but a prison cell? And this place, with its stately brick walls, winding pathways, and lush manicured lawns, a dump? Both of us are at the exact same school, but we see it so differently.

Chapter 5

The alarm clock goes off early the next morning.

"Too soon," Kareem groans. He burrows deeper into the sheets.

I stifle a yawn as I sit up. I went straight to bed after speaking with my mother last night, but I tossed and turned for hours. It's not that the bed was uncomfortable. The thick, padded mattress was softer than my woven charpay at home. But it wasn't *my* bed. And then there were all the unfamiliar noises, like the creaking pipes and the low roar of the air-conditioning.

There was also the problem of my mind refusing to turn off. How hard would classes be? Would I get laughed off the field at soccer tryouts? And my mother . . . was she lying awake, too, in our newly empty home?

I rub my eyes and get out of bed. If astronauts can fall asleep in zero gravity, I should be able to get used to my new bed and the sounds of this place.

As I brush my teeth and slip into my uniform, the sleepiness vanishes. I look at myself in the mirror and grin: Navy blue jacket? Check. Striped gold tie? Double check! It's happening. After all these months of counting down, today is the first day of my new life!

Morning barrels forward at such a breakneck pace I can barely catch my breath. Back home, we had one classroom. Here we hurry from class to class as fast as we can to beat the bell. And there are *so many people* here. Elbows and shoulders knock against me as I race down the hallways. It's like trying to maneuver through the asteroid belt.

When it's finally time for lunch, I breathe a sigh of relief. The dining hall looks like the expensive restaurants I've glimpsed on TV, with its cream tablecloths and low-hanging lights. Back at my old school, we brought our food in cloth sacks and ate on the lawn beneath a shade tree.

"How is it already lunchtime?" Kareem mutters. We step into a line stretching practically to the door. "This day is going by at warp speed."

"Really? It feels like it's dragging on forever, and we're still only halfway done." Naveed adjusts his glasses. "But the teachers go so fast I can't keep up. I missed a *bunch* of things."

"Don't worry," I tell him. "We'll compare notes after school."

We reach the food, and my mouth starts to water. Sizzling trays of chicken kardhai, saag, and steaming hot rice and naans rest underneath warming lights. This spread is fancier than some wedding buffets I've been to. A friendly man with neatly parted hair replenishes the naans as I approach.

"Everything looks delicious," I tell him.

"Doesn't *taste* too bad either." He winks. "Enjoy."

I thank him and fill my plate.

The three of us settle down at an empty table by the back doors.

"Finally!" Kareem exclaims. "I was about to pass out from hunger."

"Is there always so much food?" I ask them. Kareem and Naveed have both been at private schools before.

"Yep!" Kareem says in between shoveling food into his mouth. "And this chicken is amazing! Miles better than the eats we had at my other school."

"Did you both get the email from the guidance counselor, Mrs. Rashid?" Naveed asks between bites.

"You mean the questionnaire with about five hundred prompts?" Kareem asks.

"Twenty-three," Naveed corrects him. "She said we could schedule an appointment to see her if we need extra help."

"Right." Kareem snorts. "Nice try."

"What do you mean?" I ask.

"Take it from me," he says. "The guidance counselor at my old school tried that. You can't let them see you sweat. Don't give them a reason to say you don't belong. As far as Mrs. Rashid goes, everything is always going great."

"Are you sure?" Naveed frowns. "The handbook said she'll email each month to check in on our progress."

"One hundred percent positive." Kareem grabs his water and gulps it down. "Just hope she's not sending us those long questionnaires each time. Like we don't have enough to do."

I pull out a notebook and jot down a reminder to set up my email. I'm only halfway through the day and the list of things to do keeps growing.

A bell trills outside the door.

"And that's that." Kareem tosses his napkin onto his tray.

"Time's up? Already?" I stare at him. "I've barely touched my food."

"Twenty-five minutes goes fast," Naveed says.

"They should call it the food Olympics." Kareem glances at my plate. "Omar, you'll have to pick up your time if you want to make the cut!"

I look at my plate. Twenty-five minutes to get in line, grab our food, *and* eat? I wolf down a few bites as fast as I can before returning my tray.

"Hey, Omar!" Marwan calls out. He's with Naveed's roommate, Jibril. "Soccer was awesome yesterday! Rematch after school?"

"Definitely!" I reply.

"Speed up!" Kareem urges me and Naveed as we jostle through the crowds. I look back at Jibril's and Marwan's retreating figures. They've been in almost all my other classes, but I guess we're in different English sections.

"Why'd they put this class so far apart from the others?" I groan.

"What kind of soccer skills can you have if you're tired after a little jog?" Kareem teases. "Last one left complaining is the loser."

"Never!" I pick up my pace.

"Think Aiden'll be in this class, too?" Naveed asks. "I don't know why, but he makes me nervous."

I bite back a laugh. *Everything* makes Naveed nervous. But he's right. Aiden's been in almost every section we had. He barely speaks, but his presence is like a black hole swirling in the back of each class.

"Are we going the right way?" I ask. "This is far!"

"I haven't been in this wing either." Naveed checks the schedule. "It says 'Administrative Room Three.'"

Maybe there's a misprint, I'm about to say when we reach the assigned room.

"Did one of you ring the fire alarm or something?" Kareem asks. "Because it looks like we're heading into detention."

"Yeah," I say. "The main office is right next door."

The late bell sounds as we step inside. The space is smaller than any of the other classrooms. There are a few desks and an oak table with a swiveling chair at the front of the room. Standing next to it is the teacher.

Or—I realize—*not* a teacher. I recognize him from the photo in the welcome letter in our student folder. He's Headmaster Moiz. The head of our school. He wears a gray suit. His arms are folded. He looks like he's never smiled a day in his life.

He studies us silently, and now I'm wondering if Kareem's right. *Are* we in trouble?

"Timeliness is of utmost importance," he finally says. His voice echoes off the back wall. "We cannot expect to be taken seriously if we don't show our teachers the respect they deserve. Part of respect is arriving where expected on time."

"Sorry." Naveed's face is the color of a ripe tomato. "W-we won't be late again."

My cheeks burn as we take our seats. It's our first day of school! No one else said a word when other students stumbled in a little late. But I'm pretty sure saying any of this will only get us in more trouble.

"As you may know, I'm Headmaster Moiz," he says. "This year, I will also be teaching English to the scholarship students."

Kareem and I glance at each other. He raises his eyebrows.

"I hope a more tailored approach will provide better outcomes this year," he continues. "English is where kids like you are most deficient."

Kids like us? He said it like we're invading aliens.

He goes over his expectations, but before I can scrawl any of it down, he's passing out assignments for the week. I try to keep up with everything he's saying. Weekly quizzes. Monthly tests. Essays. All our other teachers just handed out class descriptions and asked us to introduce ourselves. Does he think this is our only class?

When I look up, Headmaster Moiz is looking right at me.

"Is there a problem?" he asks.

I shift under his piercing gaze.

"No, sir," I manage to respond.

"I should hope not," he says. "It's your first day. It only gets more complicated from here."

He turns to the whiteboard and starts to jot down the spelling words for the week. I push away the sinking feeling that washes over me. We've been here less than five minutes, but I can tell the headmaster's already decided he does not like me. But teachers always like me! It's not like I'm a genius, but I'm responsible. I work hard and get excellent grades.

I copy the spelling words and remind myself it's only the first day of school. Even if I didn't make the best first impression, I'm going to do so well in this class, he'll change his mind and see he was wrong about me.

Chapter 6

Mr. Adeel holds the door wide open for art class with a smile that's even wider. His bow tie is fantastic: green with yellow polka dots.

"Omar, great to see you!" he says.

After Headmaster Moiz's class, Mr. Adeel's kindness is like an oxygen tank in outer space. He was our orientation guide over the summer and is easily the nicest teacher I've ever had. At least I'll be ending each school day on a happy note.

The walls inside the classroom are filled with art prints. There's a Hall of Fame board with artwork by previous students on the back wall, and papier-mâché trees hang from the ceiling. The open space behind our desks is crowded with easels, baskets of beads, and other art supplies stacked on shelves. Paint-spattered smocks hang on hooks along the wall. Even Aiden's negative energy wafting over like fog from the back of the room feels muted here.

Mr. Adeel dims the lights and flips on a projector.

"This semester we're exploring art movements as a tool for change. And next semester you'll make an art project of your own!"

"Fun!" Humza exclaims. Other kids murmur excitedly.

I sink in my seat. An art project sounds like the exact opposite of fun. I can't remember the last time I tried to draw anything. I'm no artist. I have no idea how I will catch up to people who've taken courses like these their whole lives. But as I sit back and look at the slides flashing on the screen, I'm amazed at all the different art forms: paintings, statues, murals, and large-scale art installations. I feel myself relax a little.

"Many artists work in response to the times they live in," Mr. Adeel says. "They aim to evoke a response. It could be awe, discomfort, or even repulsion, but the goal is to make you *feel*. It's why art is a great way to shed light on important social justice issues. At the end of the year, you'll also be presenting on an artist of your choice, so make note of the ones who speak to you."

Speak to us? The pictures on the screen are interesting, but none of them speak to me. Or maybe I just can't hear them.

"How's your first day going?" Mr. Adeel asks me when the bell rings and we start to leave.

"It's been nonstop," I admit. "There's so much information to process, it's like I'm already behind."

"Trust me, you're not the only one feeling that way. Just 'fake it till you make it.' You'll get there. And remember, the first week is toughest. It gets easier from here." He glances at the wall clock and grimaces. "Quick favor? I have a meeting I need to jet to in five minutes. Since you're done for the day, mind leaving this file at the front desk for me?"

"Of course." I take a manila folder from him.

Fake it till you make it. I turn Mr. Adeel's words over as I walk to the administrative wing. Kids hurry past me. They're laughing and chatting as they head toward the dorms. Are they faking it? Doesn't look like it to me.

Stepping into the administrative office, my feet sink into carpeting so plush, it's like I'm walking on clouds. As I set the file on the counter, a deep voice booms from down the hallway. Headmaster Moiz. I know he's not going to burst forth from his office like a gust of wind and drag me inside to berate me, but the sooner I leave the better.

Returning to the hallway, I hear a laugh that sounds like Kareem's. I frown. All the way here?

But there it is again. Kareem. His voice is coming from a narrow corridor to my left. Craning my neck, I see him by an open door. His back is to me.

"I know. I know. Study like your life depends on it," he says. "Got it." He pauses. I hear a muffled response. "Yes, Abu! I swear I'm eating properly!"

Abu? What is Kareem's father doing here?

A man emerges from behind the doorway. I take a quick step back, out of sight. Peering from the edge, I see he has wavy brown hair like Kareem.

I turn and hurry the opposite way, taking the long way to the dorms so they don't spot me.

My head spins. Kareem's father is at Ghalib. He never said anything about it to me. Why is he keeping it a secret?

Chapter 7

The soccer field is the best thing about Ghalib, but the rec room's a close second. Stepping inside after dinner tonight feels like the perfect way to cap off my first day. Two boys from biology are playing foosball in the back of the room next to Jibril and Marwan, who are battling it out on the Ping-Pong table. A few kids sit at a table by a bay window, their eyes fixed to glowing tablets in their hands.

I settle down on a sofa across from a sleek black TV hanging on the wall, right next to Naveed and Humza, who are fighting for the remote. I stifle a laugh. Their scuffles for the remote were a regular fixture during orientation weekend, too.

"That's it. Omar decides!" Humza tosses the remote to me. "What do you pick? Soccer or *Maheen Matters*?"

"She's the one who gives out the advice you're always sharing, right, Naveed?" I ask.

"*Cheesy* advice!" Humza interjects.

Naveed gives an exaggerated gasp. "It's so not cheesy."

"Sorry, but Humza's right," Marwan calls out from the back of the room.

"It's a thirty-minute episode," Naveed protests. "Your game will still be going on and no one will have probably scored a point anyway."

They watch me, a kid who only ever rarely glimpsed a TV back home, like the fate of the world rests on my shoulders.

"I'll go with *Maheen Matters*," I finally say.

"You can't be serious!" Humza gasps.

Naveed grabs the remote from me and holds it up like it's a trophy. He flips through the channels until a woman appears. She's sitting across from a man in a blue shirt and dark jeans. "I'm here with Feroz Hashim. He's joining us to share his acting journey and how he became the person he is today."

"Yeah, right, this is way better than soccer." Humza sulks.

Feroz talks about the auditions he's bombed. The struggles to define his acting career.

36

"I finally decided to stop chasing the jobs I thought I needed to go for the ones I really connected with. It's like that line in *Hamlet*," Feroz tells Maheen. " 'To thine own self be true.' And then just like that, I got my big break. And the rest"—he laughs—"is history."

"Feroz is living proof of what I always tell my viewers," Maheen says. "Work hard on what you truly believe in and persevere. If you do, anything is possible."

"See?" Naveed says triumphantly. "That was some good advice, wasn't it?"

"Naveed." Kareem walks in and settles onto the arm of the sofa as a commercial comes on. "This stuff rots your brain."

"Is that why she's got the number one talk show in the country?" Naveed counters, crossing his arms.

I bite back a laugh. Naveed second-guesses himself about pretty much everything, but apparently not about Maheen. I study Kareem's profile. I haven't seen him since I stumbled upon him earlier today. Did he see me before I hurried away? If he did, I can't tell.

"Speaking of Shakespeare." Humza leans back. "Omar, do you have Mr. Mattu for English?"

"He's the best!" Marwan exclaims. "We're going to watch the film version of *Macbeth* once we finish reading the play."

My face grows warm. How do I explain that the head of our school is also my English teacher? Before I can think of how to respond, the show resumes.

"Whoa, is that Daniyal Mahmood?" Marwan exclaims. "My dad flew me and my cousins to Karachi to see him in concert last month. He's so good!"

Naveed beams like he invited Daniyal onto the show himself, and I'm relieved everyone's forgotten about English teachers.

Daniyal strums his guitar, and the music is catchy; even the kids over at the table slip off their earbuds to listen. Marwan asks me to play Ping-Pong with him. I've never played before, but I get the hang of it pretty easily.

Maybe Ghalib will be like this, too. Maybe I'll get the hang of all of this. Maybe it's only a matter of time.

Chapter 8

Lights flicker on around the field as I play soccer with my friends.

"Omar! Humza's on your tail!" shouts Marwan.

I kick the ball with all the force I can muster. It whips into the air full speed toward the soccer net. Jibril dives for it, but the ball ricochets off the net.

"How did you *do* that?" Jibril kicks up the ball and cradles it under his arm. "I could've sworn you were aiming to the right."

"Fake-out," I reply.

"You haven't done a fake-out all week!" Humza exclaims. "You have to know *when* to do it, or it won't work!"

"Not to be a downer, but are you *sure* we're allowed to

play soccer this late?" Naveed glances around. "We're the only ones out here."

"It's Friday! Lights-out is later on the weekends, remember? Besides, did you hear anything that says we couldn't?" Humza asks.

"Well, no—" Naveed begins.

"We're allowed to have a life outside of studying. I think even Maheen would agree!" Humza playfully punches Naveed on the shoulder. "You worry too much!"

I feel a pang of sympathy for Naveed. If worrying was a sport, Naveed would be a world champion. I glance at the mural along the edge of Ghalib Academy. Closer up, I see that there are graduation caps lining the top and that some of the mural's paint is peeling. Parts of my favorite portion, with the telescope, are discolored from the beating sun. I know everyone who has a window facing this side of the school can see the telescope as easily as me, but when I look at it from my desk when I'm studying, it feels like it's there just for me. A sign from the universe to keep at it.

"Have you seen Kareem?" Marwan asks. "He missed soccer yesterday, too."

"I looked for him in the library," Naveed says.

"He probably went back to work in our room," I say quickly, and try to change the subject. "Did you see the

40

email we got about assembly on Monday? We get to join clubs after that."

"Omar, we have to try out for soccer!" Marwan says.

"I'm signing up for chess," Naveed says. "I beat all my cousins at it back home, even the older ones. They get so mad when a kid beats them."

"Remind me not to play you." I laugh. "Sure. I'll try out for soccer, Marwan. And I'm definitely joining the astronomy club."

"Astronomy sounds fun," Humza says wistfully. "Not sure I'll have room after all the clubs I *have* to sign up for."

"Are there required clubs?" Naveed asks.

"Required by my dad. I have to join debate. And newspaper. He was the editor back when he was a student here."

"My dad's *also* making me sign up for newspaper." Marwan makes a face.

"It's like they want us to be their clones," Humza complains.

Listening to them, I think about my own dad, who died when I was a baby. I don't know much about him, but he probably couldn't ever have imagined me at a school like this; I hope he'd be proud. Watching my new friends complaining, I think about how different we are. For them, Ghalib is a given. It's part of their family legacy.

For me, it's a life raft. Still, I make a mental note to look into the newspaper club. If their parents think they should join, they probably have a good reason.

"What're they doing?" Naveed points to a group of students putting folding chairs on the lawn near the gym and setting up a wheeled machine with a glass top.

"Friday movie night, remember?" Humza says. "Let's grab some front-row seats."

As we walk over, popping noises come from the machine, and a buttery scent fills the air. Of course this school would even have popcorn on movie night!

"Hey!" Kareem jogs over to us. "Glad we all got here early for this."

"At last, the mystery man arrives," Humza remarks. "Busy fighting crime? You missed soccer again!"

"Oh, sorry." Kareem blushes. "I was—I was at the library."

Naveed frowns. "I swung by earlier but didn't see you."

"Probably just missed each other," I say. "So much work to do, I should've been there, too."

"Classes are brutal," Humza says. "Most of the teachers seem to think they're the only ones giving us work."

"Yes!" An ounce of relief creeps in. Humza's been attending schools like these his whole life, and he also thinks it's a lot.

Grabbing a seat, I spot Aiden. He's standing on the walkway by the dorms, watching the gathering crowd. But he doesn't join us. Instead, he stalks back toward our building.

"Social as always." Humza snorts, following my gaze.

"He hasn't said a word in any class I have with him," Marwan says.

"So he doesn't just look down on us scholarship kids, huh?" Naveed says.

I wince. It's not that our being here on scholarship is a secret, exactly, but it is the first time it's been said aloud. I study Humza's, Jibril's, and Marwan's expressions. None of them react to this new information.

"Guess he's an equal opportunity hater." Humza shrugs.

"Yeah, and he thinks this place is a dump, so that must make all of us a little dumpish," Kareem says.

"Is *dumpish* an actual word?" Naveed frowns.

"Not yet, but new words crop up every day," Kareem replies. "You watch, Aiden'll petition for it to be in the official dictionary."

I settle down next to them, and relief floods my system. No one seems to care we're scholarship students. Naveed brings over a paper bag filled with popcorn and a tin full of triangle-shaped snacks—which I learn are nachos.

I've never had anything quite like it before—all cheesy and salty and delicious.

Every seat is full by the time the movie starts. The crowd stops talking, and I can feel the excitement. This is what I was hoping it'd be like here, and for now I don't feel the ache of homesickness.

I look back at our dorm building. The light in the room next to ours turns on. Aiden really is a swirling dark cloud, but I can't help feeling a little sorry for him. He's the one missing out.

Chapter 9

I'm sleepy." Kareem yawns as we grab seats in the auditorium for our first assembly.

There's a podium set up on the stage, and behind it a screen flashes images of smiling students wearing the same uniforms as we do. I glance down at my shiny tie. My mother made me practice tying it so many times my hands ached, but even as I start my second week here, I don't understand why this strip of fabric is so important.

"I was so scared I'd be late!" Naveed says, taking a seat next to me. "There aren't enough sinks and showers for all of us, and Aiden was taking *forever* at the last sink even though it was obvious he was done."

"Doesn't shock me," I say.

"Just another entitled rich boy." Kareem shrugs. "Schools like this are full of them."

"How's Jibril as a roommate?" I ask Naveed. "You guys getting along?"

"He's fine, except for the mornings," Naveed says. "If I ask him anything, he looks like he'll bite my head off."

"Sounds like he's not a morning person. I'm not really either," I tell Naveed. "Besides, you're basically the perfect roommate. You keep that place so neat, you could eat off the floor!"

"Yeah, we'd have trouble *finding* our floor." Kareem laughs. "Maybe Omar and you should trade places for a while!"

"It's not that bad!" I protest. "Is it?"

"Nah, I'm just messing with you." Kareem grins.

"Well, consider yourself lucky to have a quiet roomie, Naveed." Humza leans in from the seat behind us. "Marwan's nice and all, but he talks nonstop. Did you know he has four cats back home? Two parakeets? He skis with his parents every winter in the Swiss Alps and flies there in the family jet. I think I might know his height, weight, and blood type by now."

I laugh, but before I can reply, the lights dim. The chatter fades. Headmaster Moiz walks up to the podium.

"To our students, both returning and new, welcome." His gravelly voice booms out of the microphone. "As an alumni of this fine academy, it is a great pleasure to welcome the future generation of the brightest and best our country has to offer."

An alumni? I blink at this new information. It's hard to imagine him my age, wearing a uniform and sitting in one of these seats.

The headmaster introduces us to the deputy headmaster, who's as stern looking as he is; the bursar, Mr. Rashid; and his wife, Mrs. Rashid, the guidance counselor. I recognize her from student registration day. Headmaster Moiz fills us in on the school's expectations and our responsibilities.

"And finally, that brings me to the topic I know you are all waiting to hear about: extracurriculars," the headmaster says.

Extracurriculars! At this, I perk up. My mind buzzes with all the possibilities. Astronomy club's a given, and I've been eager to check out archery ever since Amal mentioned it.

"The gymnasium next door is set up with Ghalib's offerings, but before I dismiss you, if your student folder had the letters *SB* on it, you won't be heading there quite yet, so please remain seated."

SB. Those two letters were stamped on my folder. When Mrs. Rashid handed it to me on arrival day, she told me not to worry about it. But now I can't help but worry as I watch everyone get up to leave. Soon only about a dozen of us remain. Besides Kareem and Naveed, I recognize a couple of faces, including Faisal, the boy who helped me punch in the dorm code.

"We're in trouble. We are. I know it." Naveed's face is pale. "But I—I don't even know what we did?"

Before I can respond, Headmaster Moiz summons Faisal to join him onstage.

"You lot"—the headmaster tells us—"are our Scholar Boys. Thanks to the generosity of our alumni, we open up a small number of spots each year for scholarship kids like you."

Kids like us. There it is again. He makes it sound like we snuck in here without permission.

"Faisal is one of our star scholarship students." He nods to the boy. "I'm proud to say he's graduating with the highest of honors this spring. Do seek him out after we're done here. He may be able to answer your questions from a different perspective.

"Scholar Boys are required by our bylaws to complete five service hours each week," Headmaster Moiz continues. "You will receive details about this in a forthcoming email, but tasks will include chores like grounds maintenance, kitchen work, and laundry duty. As this is a significant time commitment in addition to your studies, Scholars will not participate in extracurricular clubs their first year."

What? No astronomy club? No soccer?

"But why?" I blurt out.

The headmaster turns to me. His lips press into a thin line.

"The board believes extracurriculars make it difficult for new students to stay focused on their studies. Next year, extracurriculars will be discussed on a case-by-case basis."

I sink into my seat. *It's fine*, I tell myself. It's not like the school back home would've had archery or robotics or chess club. And cleaning up after meals—it's nothing I haven't done before. It's a simple enough requirement in exchange for the chance to be here.

But it still hurts.

"I've been a headmaster for fifteen years and seen far too many Scholars stumble." Headmaster Moiz's gaze returns to me. "Some graduate and go on to do great things. Many, however, do not. I hope all of you will prove to be the exception and stay through until the very end. Be mindful of your opportunity. You are lucky boys indeed."

A burst of laughter floats into the auditorium from the gym next door.

Lucky.

What about the boys on the other side of the wall? Picking whichever activities they'd like because they were born into families who can pay their tuition.

He's right. I'm lucky. But it's hard to feel that way right now.

Chapter 10

*Y*ou coming?" Kareem asks me.

The other scholarship kids are heading to the gymnasium like the headmaster instructed us to once he wrapped up his talk. But I can't move. Why would I go there? To look at what I can't have?

"I'm going back to my room," I finally say.

"Are you sick?" Naveed asks worriedly.

"I'm not sick . . ." My voice trails off. At summer orientation we toured the campus and our future classrooms. We were told all about Ghalib's stellar reputation, but why weren't we oriented to the fact that scholarship kids would be second-class citizens?

I look at Naveed and Kareem. They're waiting for me. Maybe it's better to shrug it off and go along with them. But I don't trust that I won't start blubbering when I see all the activities I can't be part of.

"Don't worry, we'll cover for you," Kareem says. "I'm just peeking in to see if they'll let us shoot some hoops."

I watch them leave the auditorium. I take a few deep breaths. I have to leave eventually. I have to get going.

When I step into the hallway, a voice calls out.

"Careful!"

It's Kareem's father. He holds a mop, and his clothes are splattered with paint.

"Watch your step. Floor's damp from a spill I just mopped up."

"Oh. Thanks," I tell him. "I'm Omar."

"Omar." He smiles. "Nice to meet you. You're new, right?"

"Yes," I say.

"I'm Zamir. If you ever need anything, I'm always around somewhere, fixing whatever needs fixing."

He nods at me and sticks his mop in his bucket, rolling it down the hallway. His easy smile, the light brown of his eyes—he's a bigger version of Kareem. And he's a janitor here at Ghalib. Is that why Kareem kept it a secret? Does he worry people will think less of him? I wonder if his father knows who I am, or if Kareem's kept me a secret, too.

The doors to the gym are pushed open when I pass by, and even though I know I shouldn't, I can't help it. I look in. Tables for the various activities are set out along the perimeter of the room, and it's packed with kids milling around. A banner hangs from one of the tables with the words *Model United Nations*. Next to it, the band crew proudly displays tubas and trombones alongside instruments I don't even recognize. The robotics, newspaper, and debate clubs are lined up along the other wall. And then I see it: A sleek black telescope, a painted poster board with glittering planets and meteors. Astronomy club. Humza leans down, writing his name on a sheet on the table.

My mother had teased me, saying that I'd be like Safa let loose in a candy store here. She shouldn't have worried. I'm on the outside looking in while everyone else eats to their heart's content.

I spot Kareem at the far side of the gym, playing basketball with a group of kids. He shoots the ball straight into the net. The kids around him cheer. Kareem grins and takes a deep bow. I swallow. Why can't I get on with things like him? The news from today doesn't change the fact that this school is the key to unlocking a new destiny. But even as I tell myself this, tears fill my eyes. I take another deep breath. I can't cry. Not here.

"Hey." Faisal is suddenly at my side. "You okay?"

I clear my throat. "Yeah. I just . . . I didn't know about the extracurricular thing. Or the chores. It's no big deal. I'm glad to be here. But—"

"But it's still a punch to the gut, isn't it?"

"Yeah." My jaw unclenches a little.

"But Headmaster Moiz is right," he says. "Your first year is really tough."

"Isn't it hard for *everyone*?"

"It's . . . it's different for us," he says. "But on the bright side, they let you sign up for whatever you want after your first year. I'm on the track team. Newspaper. I even tried archery last semester."

So it really is just this year. My shoulders relax a little.

"If you ever have questions about how Ghalib works, you can always ask me," he says.

"I do have one question. How do chores work?"

"They're annoying, but not so bad," he says. "You can do stuff like fold towels and linens in the laundry room, that's a cinch. Dishes—washing, drying, putting them away—that's a breeze, too."

"Is that what you do?"

"I try to get chores done first thing in the morning," he says. "Shuaib and Basem, the cooks, can always use extra help doing morning prep. Washing and chopping things."

"And it keeps you behind the scenes." That's another part of the equation hitting me. If Humza and the others didn't care that we were scholarship kids, they might feel differently if they see me taking out the trash.

Faisal studies me. "It stings a little at first," he says gently. "Not going to lie about that. But it gets easier."

He's saying this to make me feel better. He has to be. How can it ever feel easier to be treated like a second-class student?

• • •

When I punch in the dorm code and push the door open, it bumps against something.

"Hey! Watch it."

I realize quickly it's a some*one*. Aiden. He glares at me, his phone in his hand.

"Sorry," I begin. "I didn't—"

"Yeah, you sure didn't, charity case."

Without another word, he walks up the stairs.

Charity case.

The words land like a slap. He said it like having a scholarship means I'm not part of the same species. I guess to him, I'm not.

I think of the going-away party at Amal's house. The laughter. The hugs. The desserts. Everyone had chipped in to buy me a leather bag that they presented to me in shiny gold wrapping.

Back home, everyone was proud of me.

Back home, everyone was jostling for me to be part of their team.

But I'm not home now.

Chapter 11

By the time the lights-out bell sounds on our floor that night, I'm ready to pass out. But as quickly as I close my eyes, they spring open. Chores. I completely forgot.

Kareem's back is toward me, and he's lightly snoring. I want to sleep so badly, but I can't fall behind. Not this early into the school year. Sitting up, I slip on my sandals and pad to the end of the hallway to our floor's laundry room. Folding and sorting sounds like a simple enough way to get in my hours if there's anything there to take care of.

Entering the room, a fluorescent tube overhead buzzes before turning on, revealing three large washers and dryers and a metal counter with a pile of folded towels. I open a dryer. A batch of warm towels are bundled inside.

Pulling them onto the counter, I start folding. Squaring the edges, setting each one to the side. There are so many people who keep this school running. Gardeners. Cooks. Maintenance people. I even saw some housekeepers gathering towels in the bathroom just this morning. They don't *need* us to do this work. They want to make sure we remember our place.

My thoughts drift to Kareem. He helped me troubleshoot my email this afternoon. We talked about our classes over dinner. But he never mentioned his father. Not once. I understand him not wanting to broadcast that information to the world, but why wouldn't he tell *me*?

"Hey."

I nearly jump out of my skin at the unexpected voice. Naveed. He stands at the entrance of the laundry room. His hair's matted, and he holds his hand up to cover a yawn.

"Couldn't sleep either, huh?" I ask.

"I know this is weird," he says. "But the bed is almost . . . *too* soft?"

"Yes! I was thinking the same thing."

"And I guess we both thought we could find something to do here for our service hours. I don't want to get in trouble for falling behind."

"Great minds think alike." I gesture to the towels. "Plenty for both of us."

We get to work pulling all the clean towels from the other dryers to fold, and I tell Naveed about my encounter with Faisal. "He told me he likes to help in the kitchen. Cutting up stuff and washing dishes."

"That's a logical plan," he says. "We can get it all done before classes even start. Maheen always says success comes to those who seize the day."

"Still"—I hesitate—"it kind of stinks, doesn't it?"

"No," he says without missing a beat. "It *definitely* stinks."

We don't say much more after that. We fold and stack until all the towels are neatly pressed into squares on the metal rack along with the other clean towels.

It's not fun to have to do this. But it helps not being in it alone.

Chapter 12

Up early, huh?" Faisal says as Kareem, Naveed, and I
step into the kitchen behind the dining hall. He has on an
apron and stands in front of a cutting board, slicing apples.
"Wash up and grab an apron."

As we wash our hands, the door swings open again. Two
men, one with a bushy gray mustache and neatly parted
hair, and a younger one, enter. I recognize them from our
meals; they always come and go mostly unnoticed, replen-
ishing trays.

Faisal introduces us. The older man nods. "Great to
meet you. Name's Shuaib. Head cook. And this is Basem."

Our task is simple. Chop fruit for breakfast and place

it in serving tins. Slice vegetables for the cooks to prepare for lunch.

"Faisal is a pro at getting his work done as efficiently as possible," Shuaib says. He pulls out a vat of flour and pours it into a larger mixer. "Sometimes he knocks out all his hours for the week in one day."

"I usually do that when midterms or finals are coming up," Faisal says.

As we slice and chop, the kitchen comes to life with conversation. Naveed nervously peppers Faisal with questions about how tough the history teacher really is, while the cooks gossip about the new swim coach.

I glance around, taking in my surroundings. Everything here is shiny and metallic. Even the counters and the wide sinks on opposite ends of the room gleam. But as different as it all is, there's something familiar about it. The way the cooks joke with each other and us. The sounds of washing and chopping vegetables. It's comfortable. It reminds me of home.

"What's your favorite subject so far?" Naveed asks as we put away bowls of honeydew and berries.

"Math," Kareem says. "It's the easiest by a mile."

"Math is okay, but I like art," says Naveed. "Mr. Adeel is so nice. And we get to paint in a few weeks."

"Adeel's nice and all," Kareem says. "But his slideshows make me want to nap. What's *your* favorite class, Omar?"

"I think Moiz is the one to beat for the title of absolute favorite teacher, don't you guys?"

Naveed's eyes widen—then he howls with laughter.

"Honestly?" I continue. "I think he's part grizzly bear."

"Yeah, he really loves us scholarship kids, doesn't he," Faisal says.

"Well, it could always be worse," Kareem says. "At my last school, we had this one teacher who made us write 'I will not be late' one hundred times on the chalkboard for every minute we were tardy."

I guess Kareem's right. It could always be worse. But studying my cutting board, I wonder: Isn't it okay sometimes to be disappointed in what is?

Aiden's words for us flash in my mind. *Charity case.* Even now, the words burn. I know he's an entitled jerk who thinks this school with its enormous pool and horse stables is a dump. But he is right about me. I *am* here on charity. I think about Marwan, who flies to a different continent so he can ski down a snowy mountainside. Practically everyone here has their own laptop and smartphone, so they never have to set foot in the computer lab if they don't want to.

I've always known I'm poor, but until Ghalib, I never *felt* poor.

"This was way better than folding towels in the dead of night," Naveed says, untying his apron.

"Folding towels at night?" Faisal asks. "I hope that's not what you just said."

"We didn't want to fall behind on chores," I tell him. "There were towels in the dryer last night, so Naveed and I got to work."

The chefs grow quiet.

Faisal lowers his knife. "Do you know how much trouble you could get into for being out of your rooms after lights-out?"

"But . . . we were doing chores." Naveed's expression grows pale. "We're supposed to do five hours a week."

"Lights-out are lights-out. Don't ever do that again." Basem shakes his head. "Good thing the warden didn't do a random check of your floor and find you. Last thing you want is to get yourself kicked out before you've even really started."

A chill goes through me. Kicked out?

"And those hours won't even count," Faisal continues. "There has to be a staff person supervising to sign off on your hours. Can't exactly ask anyone to sign off on work you did after-hours. You should have gotten an email with all the details. You better read it."

My cheeks flush. Why *hadn't* I read the email yet? It was the first thing I should have done. The first thing I *will* do this afternoon.

"Don't worry." Shuaib swats my arm kindly. "Bring the sheet tomorrow and we'll sign off for today."

"I can't believe last night won't count." Naveed groans. "We folded all that laundry for nothing."

"Consider yourself lucky you didn't get caught." Basem chuckles.

But nothing about this is funny. How could a school so hard to get into be so easy to get thrown out of?

Chapter 13

Kareem, you did the best of the lot, although that's not saying much," Headmaster Moiz says, handing us back the results of our latest essay. Three weeks into the school year, I knew better than to hope for an A in this class, but another C scrawled across the page still stings.

Naveed's mark must be just as bad. "Sorry," he says. "I—I'll try to bring my grades up."

"I should hope so," the headmaster replies. "The further into the year we go, the less room we have for mistakes as simple as these. I suggest both you and Omar take this class a bit more seriously."

More seriously? I jerk my head up. Is he being sarcastic?

It feels like all I do is schoolwork. How much more seriously can I possibly take it?

He turns his back to us and begins writing on the board. I grip the edge of my desk until my knuckles go white. Is it a coincidence the class I struggle most in is the one where the teacher clearly doesn't believe in us?

All my classes are harder than back home, but no other teachers treat us like this. Earlier today, I got an A in biology class. Mr. Nawaz scrawled the words *Impressive improvement!* beneath it.

Can I ever catch up in a class where the teacher thinks I'm not good enough to even be here?

• • •

"Hey! Easy there. What did those onions ever do to you?"

Shuaib puts a hand on my shoulder the next morning. I look down and see indentations on the cutting board from my blows.

"Sorry," I tell him. "Was thinking about English class. It's just . . . it feels impossible."

"It sure does," Naveed says. He's across from me, slicing tomatoes.

"Headmaster Moiz isn't much of a picnic, is he?" Shuaib says. "Don't know what got into him wanting to teach

66

a class after all these years. He's bound to have gotten rusty."

"He was a teacher?" Naveed asks.

"Yep. Taught English when I started here," Shuaib says. "Guess he got nostalgic and thought he'd take a stab at it again."

"Or maybe he wants to take a stab at *us*," I mutter. "He's out to get us. Or at least, out to get *me*."

"Now, why would he be out to get you?" Shuaib asks.

"All I know is that no matter how hard I work in that class, my grades stay stuck. It's starting to feel hopeless."

"Hopeless?" he scoffs. "The Lahore Sikanders are hopeless at cricket. Yasin Ullah's bowling average is *absolutely* hopeless. But this? Sure, it's hard, but you're smart enough to figure it out. Look at Faisal. He's been where you are, and now he's almost flying the coop. It won't be easy, but there's no reason you won't be like him, right, Faisal?"

"Well, Headmaster was never my teacher. And English is hard for many people . . . Learning all the rules is brutal," Faisal says somberly. "It takes time to get the hang of it."

I appreciate everything they're saying, but I'm not sure I'll ever get the hang of this. An essay isn't the same as a linear equation, where there's only one absolute right answer. Whether or not my essay is excellent depends on what Moiz thinks about it—and he's no fan of mine.

"Now listen, you're becoming one of the best prep cooks I've ever had. And you followed my directions for making the raita to perfection yesterday." Shuaib smiles at me. "Just take it easy on my utensils going forward."

"Yeah, let's not worry so much," Naveed says. "I'm scared, too. But we'll get there."

I wince. I must really seem like a mess if Naveed is comforting *me*.

"Anyone mind grabbing the trays out front so we can start filling them?" Basem asks. "The breakfast crowd should start filtering in by the end of the hour."

"Sure." I set my knife on the cutting board and head out to grab the trays from the warming bar. I'm stacking them up when the cafeteria door swings open. It's Jibril. My entire body freezes. It's like my heart's stopped beating.

"Hey, Omar." He yawns. "Up early, too?" He eyes the trays in my arms and asks, "Whatcha doing?"

"Nothing much . . . Uh, just helping the cooks."

"But there's no community service for our year, is there?" Jibril looks puzzled.

"Um. Well, there is for some of us. Kind of." Before he can interrogate me further, I rush back to the kitchen.

I try to catch my breath as I put the trays on the counter. I drop my apron on the hook on the back wall. I wash and dry my cutting board and knife. *Relax*, I tell myself. But I can't push away Jibril's baffled expression.

The gulf between me and the other students seems to grow bigger and bigger every day. Faking it until I make it is starting to feel like trying to fire a rocket ship to the edge of the ever-unfolding universe. Impossible.

Chapter 14

My art teacher, Mr. Adeel, is hands-down my favorite teacher, but PE is my favorite class. And this week's sport? Soccer!

Black-and-white balls trapped in a net dangle from Coach Zulfi's arms as he approaches us at the metal bleachers. We've learned about cricket, basketball, field hockey. Last week we tried baseball; it was okay. But soccer is different. Soccer is home. You don't need protective eyewear or a metal bat or a mouth guard or a helmet. You don't even really *need* to buy a fancy netted goal. You just need a ball. It's as simple and perfect as that.

The ground beneath me feels familiar as we follow Coach onto the field. I tap my feet while the coach goes over the rules. Then he divides us into teams by last names. Half of the class is on the blue team. I'm on the red team with Kareem and Naveed and Humza. Corresponding bandannas wrapped around our arms set us apart. When I see Aiden tie his blue bandanna on, I exhale the littlest bit. We're not on the same team.

Coach blows a whistle and we're off. Dribbling. Passing. Kicking.

The blue team is good. Really good. Most of their players are bigger than us, too.

But I'm faster.

I score once. And again. When I hit the ball with my foot, it lands in the net like it was drawn there by a magnetic force. The goalie for the other team can't stop my kicks. Marwan follows me like a shadow. But he can't outrun me. I dribble and pass the ball to my teammates. I steal it from the other team.

The sun beats down on us. Sweat trickles down my nose. But it doesn't matter. There's only one thing in the world that does: that soccer ball.

After what feels like no time at all, the coach blows the whistle. "We have a winner!" he declares. "Red team, give yourself a round of applause. Well done."

We high-five each other. Humza hugs me. Naveed slaps me on the back. This school might make me feel like I'm trying to learn a new language without a translation guide, but on this field I know I belong.

It feels good to be excellent at something again.

"Omar, a word, please?" the coach asks me as the rest of the kids head toward the gym lockers.

"I've been hoping to talk to you," he says when I approach. "I've seen you on the field after school, kicking the ball around with some of the other boys."

"Oh." I pause. Was Naveed right? *Was* it against the rules? "I'm sorry. I saw other kids playing when I first got here, so I thought—"

"It's fine," he assures me. "The fields are open for all students when they're not in use. I was impressed with your footwork out there with your friends. But today, seeing you up close . . . you're better at this than I realized. Your focus is exceptional."

"Thank you, Coach." I flush with pride. "I've been playing since I was little."

"Ever play in a league?"

"Only with my friends."

"So *that's* why you didn't sign up for tryouts," he says. "Don't worry. We don't care about your soccer résumé— we want good players. Like you."

Just like that, the warm glow inside me is extinguished.

"Thank you, Coach. I wish I could, but I can't."

"Yes, tryouts have passed. But I'm the head coach." He winks. "I can make it work."

"It's not that," I say. "I'm not allowed."

"Says who?"

"The school rules." I hesitate. "I'm here on scholarship."

"Well, what does that have to do with anything? Why should a scholarship prevent you from—" His expression shifts and he stops himself. "Oh, right. Well, it's my first year here, so what do I know. Still, makes no sense to me. If you're good at a sport, you should play it. But next year for sure, yeah? You're a natural if ever I saw one."

I thank him before crossing the grassy field toward the gym. I impressed the coach! And he was right. It *wasn't* fair. It felt good to hear a teacher say so.

"You're taking forever!" Kareem shouts. He's by the gym door, waiting.

"Coming!"

I break into a jog toward him. Passing a group of kids huddled by one of the nets, I hear them—

"That kid. That's him," one of them says. "He's *good*."

"Yeah, he stole the ball from Marwan like it was nothing!"

I recognize two of them from biology. They usually never acknowledge I exist, but right now they're looking straight at me. The third kid is Aiden.

"Hey," one of them says. "You were good out there."

"Not bad," the other one says.

"Yeah, for a charity case, he's okay." Aiden kicks the dirt beneath him and looks the other way, while the other two boys chuckle.

Charity case. There it is again. The way he says it, it's like I'm not an actual student here.

My pace slows. I look at the mural. The telescope fixed toward the skies.

Once upon a time, there were nine planets thought to orbit the sun: Mercury, Venus, Earth, Mars, Jupiter, Saturn, Uranus, Neptune, and Pluto. But then scientists changed the rules about what made a planet and decided Pluto didn't belong. So they kicked it out. Said it wasn't a real planet anymore. Even though Pluto's still there orbiting the sun along with the others.

I guess for people like Moiz and Aiden, I'm Pluto. And they want to make sure I never forget.

Chapter 15

It's the last class on Friday, and I'm thankful the weekend's just about here.

"Parent open house is fast approaching," Mr. Adeel announces. "I'd love for us to have some art ready for your parents to see. Why don't we try out the different materials in the back of the class and see what we can come up with? Plus, it'll give you a chance to see what medium you connect with for your project. And who knows? Maybe your art piece will end up on my Hall of Fame."

"Sir . . . there's no way I can make anything like those!" Marwan points to the board. "I'm not sure what I'm even doing in a class where people could make art like that."

"Do I detect a little imposter syndrome?" Mr. Adeel asks.

"What's that?" Marwan asks.

"When you worry you're not good enough. It's common in the arts, since art is so subjective. Try not to compare yourself with others. Do your best, and the work will be its best."

Imposter syndrome. I definitely *feel* like an imposter sometimes. But this can't be a "syndrome" because my grades aren't subjective like art. They aren't open to interpretation. They're solid, undeniable letters on my papers.

The lights flick on and everyone rises from their desks.

"What movie do you think they're going to play tonight?" Marwan asks me as we head toward the back shelves. "I heard it was *Karate Kid*, but it's so *old*. I hope they go with something newer, don't you?"

I blink. I'd never seen it once, much less thought it was overplayed. "I'm—I'm not sure."

"Don't get me wrong"—he shrugs—"if they've got soda and chips, I'm there."

He hurries toward the easels at the back wall before I can answer. Which is kind of a relief, because then I don't have to be the party pooper who tells him I'm not sure I can go to movie night. The truth is, even playing soccer is kind of pushing it, considering how much work I have to catch up on.

Jibril's at the front of the class, already signing up for an artist. Humza rolls out a fist-size ball of clay and squishes it down with his hand. And Marwan's beginning to sketch something on his canvas. They're getting ready for their parents to visit and ooh and aah over their creations.

I knew the open house was fast approaching. There'd been three emails yesterday with information about visiting hours, tour schedules, and the welcome assembly. But my mother isn't coming. Even if I'd told her about it, she doesn't have a way to get here. Taking a ride on Uncle's motorcycle just isn't done. It's better she doesn't know.

I walk to the binders filled with information on the famous artists we can choose from. Aiden's flipping through one of them. Ignoring him, I grab the other one and move away. I open the book to a page filled with red dots on a white background. There are so many dots spreading out, they feel endless. It's like they extend invisibly beyond the page. I study my body for any sign of transformation. Is my soul activated? I can't tell.

"Do you like Yayoi Kusama?" Mr. Adeel asks. "We'll be talking about her in class. She likes to play with the concept of forever in her art."

I bite my lip. I'm sort of afraid to tell him, but he's been so kind . . .

"We didn't have art classes back home, so this is all new," I tell him. "But I'm thinking these circles should be easy enough to trace?"

"Kusama is a fine choice," Mr. Adeel says. "Does her work speak to you?"

"I don't know what that means, exactly . . . I guess I'm not really an art person."

"An 'art person'?" He cocks his head. "What's an 'art person'?"

"Art is great!" I say in a hurry. The last person I want to offend is my nicest teacher. "There's some cool stuff in the slides you've shown us. But I'm more of a science person. I like astronomy and stuff."

"Why can't you be a science *and* art person?" He laughs when he sees my dubious expression. "I'm serious! There are plenty who are both. And listen, don't get caught up worrying about imitating an artist, Omar. That's not what I'm looking for. I'm just hoping one of these artists will make you curious."

"It's just that I've never drawn much," I tell him.

"You don't have to draw," he says. "You could do photography. I have a camera I can loan out to you. Or you could make a collage. Try different things before settling on something."

"A collage?"

He flips through the binder. "Like these."

I frown. Some of these are made with newspaper. Cut-out letters glued together. Some have photographs snipped and arranged in unusual ways.

"This is art?" I blurt out.

"Indeed. There's much you can say by piecing things together. No matter how you go about it, I'm evaluating how well you try. Do your best."

I can do that. I can try my best. Just then, I catch sight of a poster hanging behind Mr. Adeel. The background is deep orange and in the center is a girl on a bicycle. People stare at her with shocked expressions. The girl sees these people. But her jaw stays set. She's not letting any of them stop her. I think of Hafsa from my village—she rides her bike around town all the time even though it's frowned upon for girls to ride. Like this girl, no one would dare tell Hafsa what to do.

"You like it?" Mr. Adeel nods to the poster. "Just had it framed. It's one of my favorite prints."

"The colors are so bright."

"That's her signature style. Shehzil Malik. She's from Lahore. I learned about her during the Women's March."

"Lahore? That's only an hour away from here!" Most of the other artists we've learned about lived hundreds of years ago or thousands of kilometers away. I look at the poster. "Can I choose her for my project?" I ask. "Does she do collages?"

"I don't believe she does. But you can capture the spirit of her work with a collage, I'm sure. Why don't you do some research online and see? You don't have to decide today."

I look back at the girl on the poster. The people staring her down. Judging her. I know how it feels to be surrounded by people who doubt you, but I like how this girl doesn't pay them any mind. Instead, she looks straight ahead—determined. They can think what they want; she'll do what she needs to do anyway.

Chapter 16

On the weekend of the open house, I watch as parents and grandparents stream into Ghalib's main foyer. Humza swings his little sister around. Marwan squirms against his mother's lipsticked kisses.

A lump rises in my throat. I talk to my mother a few times a week, but a phone call can't replace a hug.

"Seems like they all arrived at the exact same time, didn't they?"

I jump at the unexpected voice. It's Zamir, Kareem's father. He gestures to the crowd. "Might want to step to the side. Could get run over."

"Yeah." I force a smile.

He studies me for a moment and then—

"It's not easy, but December will be here before you know it."

I wonder how he knows my mother won't walk through those doors any moment. Is it that obvious? Or did Kareem tell him about me?

"Thanks," I tell him. "It's fine. I'm fine."

He pats my shoulder and walks away.

I know he said December's almost here to make me feel better, but it's not almost here. It's six weeks away—and it *feels* like light-years from now. I push back my homesickness. There's no point fixating on it. There's no point being sad about things you cannot change.

I watch him disappear around the corner. I think about what it's like for him. He *is* a parent of a student at this school. If Kareem wasn't keeping their relationship a secret, would they both be attending the events today like everyone else here?

When I swing by the dining hall to grab a bite to eat, I see Shuaib over by the buffet. He's balancing serving trays in one hand while yanking out burners with the other. The trays wobble dangerously. I rush in and grab them from him just in time.

"Thanks, Omar." He exhales. "Prepping for the luncheon is making my head spin."

The kitchen is sweltering when I step inside with the trays. Basem stirs three different pots on the stove. An assortment of pans and pots, still steaming, rests along the counters. A bag of onions and tomatoes lies next to a cutting board.

"Do you need help?" I ask them.

"You've already done your hours for the week," Shuaib says.

"It's okay," I tell him. "I'm happy to knead some dough or chop whatever needs chopping. Looks like you could use a hand."

"You're a genuine angel, you know that?" Shuaib pats my back. "More people than planned came, so we've been running around like chickens with their heads cut off all morning. If you could dice the onions, I'd be grateful. At the speed you work, shouldn't take long at all."

I wash my hands and start peeling and dicing. My eyes water as I chop, but I used to cut onions for my mother, so this is familiar. When I'm done, I mix up the yogurty raita and add some more salt to season it the way he likes.

"Here you go." I hand Shuaib the bowl.

He grabs a spoon and tries some. "It's official—you really *are* the best prep cook," he tells me.

"When the former head chef of one of the fanciest rest-aurants in Islamabad calls you the best *anything*, *that* is some compliment," Basem calls out. "Now, don't let it go to your head!"

"You were a chef at a restaurant?" I ask him.

"Not just any chef, he was a *celebrity* chef." Basem winks. "At Saviya. There were lines outside that place every day of the week. He's got photos with plenty of celebrities."

"I got a bit of notoriety after a critic reviewed the restaurant favorably." Shuaib laughs.

"That's the dream." Basem sighs wistfully. "Hoping I'll learn from the best and make my own way one day."

I look at Shuaib. "You left all that to come *here*?"

"Wasn't the easiest decision. But when my youngest barely knew who I was, I decided enough was enough," he says. "Besides, it's a good enough living."

"But being *famous* for your cooking. Wasn't that the dream?" I ask.

"It was nice, no denying that," he says. "But you learn there's more to life than that."

"More to life than your *dreams*?"

"Dreams can change, you know. It was hard only coming back home a few times a year."

"But leaving all that behind to work *here*?" I blurt out. "You work so hard, and the kids don't even properly appreciate you."

At this, Shuaib smiles a little. "Now, that's a big assumption, Omar. There're plenty of sweet kids here, but even if there weren't—what's it to me? The pay's good and I get to have dinner each evening with my family and tuck my kids in at night. I have no complaints."

I wash my hands and put away my apron and think about my conversation with Shuaib. I want to graduate from Ghalib. Become an astronomer. Get my mother a house. These are dreams I will never put aside, and when I make them come true, I'm holding on to them and never letting go.

Chapter 17

Why didn't you wake me up?" Kareem bursts into the library at a quarter past eleven. His shirt is untucked and his hair falls messily across his forehead.

I had just finished replying to Mrs. Rashid, after filling out the guidance counselor's monthly questionnaire. Now I was taking a break by the fiction shelf, choosing books to take home for Amal in December.

"You were knocked out," I tell him. "I don't think a rooster standing on your head would have woken you. But it's not that late. We've got plenty of time."

"Yeah?" He perks up. "Then how about shooting some hoops later today?"

"Kareem." I sigh. "I want to. But I need to study."

"You and me both. But don't they say exercise is good for the brain? Gets blood flowing or something? Come on, please? I'll be your best friend."

"Fine," I relent. "But only if we can get all the assignments we have due on Monday finished first. *Then* we'll play."

"You're tough but fair, Omar Ali." Kareem grins and pulls out his biology textbook. "And if we work twice as hard, I say we play twice the games."

I smile at him. Even though my mother isn't here, I don't feel so alone.

An hour or two into our studying, the library door swings open. Faisal and Naveed walk in and take a seat next to us.

"Your parents couldn't come today either?" I ask.

"They came once and that was enough." Faisal shrugs. "Between the bus transfers and the taxi fare . . . it didn't make sense to come back."

"My parents aren't far from here," Naveed says. "But my uncle needed the car today. It stinks, but at least we get a head start on our studying."

"Yes." Kareem groans. "*That* should make us feel better. Too bad we have a headmaster who enjoys torturing us.

No one gives as much work as he does. Did you know they watched a *movie* yesterday in Mr. Mattu's section? How is that fair?"

"He doesn't like scholarship kids," I say as my stomach lets out a huge growl.

"Your stomach agrees." Faisal laughs.

"But then why is he teaching us?" Naveed frowns.

"To remind us we're here on charity so we don't accidentally forget? Who knows," I say. "I'm not in his brain."

"I wouldn't want to be." Kareem shudders.

When my stomach rumbles for the third time, Kareem sets down his pencil. "Does your belly have something it wants to say? It's asking for attention pretty loudly."

"It's okay, Omar. I'm hungry, too," Naveed says sheepishly. "And we *have* made a dent in our work."

"Go eat," Faisal urges us. "Take a break, play basketball or something. There's no point in working yourselves to the bone over all of this. I'll watch your stuff."

• • •

There are a few other kids sitting at a table when we step inside the dining hall, including Jibril. Looks like we're not the only ones whose parents didn't come.

"Check the fridge for food," Jibril says. "The chefs just put away the banquet stuff, but they left the door open for anyone who missed it. Oh, and grab some of the yummy raita with your meal!"

We thank him and head to the back to warm up plates of rice and chicken. When I spoon raita onto my plate, I feel a swell of pride at Jibril's unknowing compliment.

Before we can sit down, the door swings open. Aiden.

"Great," I mutter under my breath.

Aiden glances around the room and then at us.

"What?" he asks gruffly.

"Me? Nothing. I—I didn't say anything," Naveed says quickly.

"You sure?" he says. "Because you all seem pretty interested in me. Staring is rude, last time I checked."

I blink. These are the most words he's ever said in my presence.

"We didn't mean to stare at you, okay?" I say. "Everyone's out with their parents, figured you would be, too."

"How about you not worry about what I'm up to?" His eyes land on Kareem. His mouth twists a little. "And, Kareem, what about you? Where are your parents?"

Kareem casts his eyes to the ground. My pulse quickens. Aiden knows.

"Oh, right. *Your* dad is here." He sneers. "I just saw him sweeping the hallway."

Kareem always has a comeback for everything, but now he's silent.

"Guess he doesn't need to go to the parent luncheon since he can just forage for leftovers in the cafeteria anytime," Aiden continues.

"You're really picking on him because his father's a janitor?" I glare at him. "He makes an honest living; that's nothing to be embarrassed by."

"True," he says. "Someone's gotta take out the trash."

"Someone does," I reply. "And I don't see your parents here at all."

"My dad can't be here because he's important," Aiden says. "Your families probably don't even have a car to get here."

"You're right. My mother doesn't have a car," I tell him. "But you were born to parents who *could* drive here but decided visiting *you* wasn't worth the effort."

"Whoa." One of the kids at the table whistles, and I hear Jibril laugh.

Aiden's mouth opens. I wait for him to lash out at me. He pauses. Then he storms away.

"Wow." Naveed exhales. "Omar. You told him!"

"Yeah," Kareem says quietly. "Thanks."

"Nice going," one of the boys at the table shouts.

"That kid's so full of it," says Jibril.

My body buzzes with energy. I'm glad Aiden's gone, and I'm glad the other kids got to see what a jerk he is.

Aiden takes this school and all his special perks as a given. Meanwhile, us scholarship kids work super-hard, just hoping to make it through.

He wants us to feel like we're outsiders. But who *really* deserves to be here more?

Chapter 18

You're fouling me!" Kareem shouts. "You can't cover me like that."

"Sorry!" I bounce the ball back to him. I'm not sure how long we've been playing, but Kareem's on a roll.

I still have a lot to learn about basketball, but Kareem's already taught me how to dribble the ball so the opponent can't steal it. How to shoot from the three-point line. How to slip past someone to make a shot.

When we finish playing, Kareem's grinning from ear to ear, and I am, too.

"You learn quick," he tells me.

"And you're *so* good," I tell Kareem. "You better try out for basketball next year."

"Sure," he says. "I'm just happy I get to play. This gym is state of the art. Maybe I should send Aiden's dad a thank-you card?"

"I'm sure he'd love that." I laugh.

"Thanks for sticking up for me earlier today," Kareem says once we're back in our room.

"Aiden's mean just to be mean," I say. "It was pretty obvious today that no one likes him."

"I was wondering when he'd say something." Kareem swallows. "He saw me with my dad a few weeks ago. Ever since then, whenever I see him in any of our classes, he smirks at me. And now, well, I guess *everyone* will know."

"It's okay, Kareem. Your dad is nice. He's not doing anything bad. It shouldn't have to be kept a secret." I pause. "Especially from me."

"I know. It's . . . it's complicated." Kareem settles down on his bed. "My dad was a janitor at my old school, too. When they ended the free tuition arrangement last summer, my dad was disappointed, but I was secretly happy. The kids there were awful." He shivers. "They never stopped going after me. Ever."

"That's awful."

"Most schools aren't like Ghalib." He shrugs. "The kids here, they're nice. Well"—he nods to the wall—"*almost* everyone . . ."

"You didn't want to risk it happening again." I get it. I remember how I tensed up when Naveed told our friends we were scholarship kids. The shame I felt when Jibril saw me holding the serving trays. But I can't imagine holding in what Kareem's been keeping inside. To walk by your parent every single day and pretend not to know them.

"I'm sorry it was so rough at the other school, Kareem. But you don't need to hide who you are here."

"No point now, anyway. Everyone's going to know the truth."

"Those kids in the cafeteria know. They didn't laugh at you," I remind him. "They laughed at Aiden. Like you said, the students here are nicer. Hopefully things will be different."

"Maybe," Kareem says.

I look at his serious expression and think about what Mr. Adeel said about faking it until you make it. Kareem always puts on a happy face. He makes jokes and shares his candy, and you'd never think he had a care in the world. But what he shows on the outside doesn't match the inside.

I'm starting to wonder if it ever does for anyone.

Chapter 19

The soccer team practices outside my bedroom window today like they do most weekday afternoons. Kareem, Naveed, and I sit on my bed studying flash cards for a quiz, but we can't help peeking down below; we have the best seats in the house.

"Jibril's stepped up his goalie skills," I say.

"Yeah, except when Marwan's kicking. With the fake-out advice you gave him, he's unstoppable these days."

"It's true," Naveed agrees. "He seems like a normal enough kid in class, but on the soccer field, I think—"

"He's part horse?" Kareem grins. "Because that has to be it."

I watch my friends on the soccer field. I'm happy they made the team, but a bubbling *want* rises up in me. I should be down there, too. Next year feels so far away.

"You want to go to the game next week?" Naveed asks. "Coach said audience participation is as important as the game itself. What if we're the only ones who don't go? Won't he get mad at us?"

"I want to go. But it'll depend how much I get done on my English essay."

"Aw, c'mon, Omar. We should go cheer them on. We don't want to let the school down, do we?" Kareem winks. "Besides, I'm getting studied out, and that's no good either."

"That's true," I say.

"Oh!" Naveed leaps up. "I forgot to tell you the news. You'll never believe it. I got a B on our last English essay!"

"Wow." I blink. "Naveed, that's amazing!"

"Amazing is right." Kareem high-fives him. "See? You're getting there!"

"It was probably a fluke." He blushes. "But it was cool to finally see a good grade."

"No fluke. You cracked Moiz's code. It's As here on out, Naveed," Kareem says.

I give him a fist bump. I'm happy for him. But now it's official: It's not impossible for scholarship students to succeed in Moiz's class. It's just impossible for *me*.

When I stand up, I look out the window and pause. The mural. It's gone. Only a faint outline remains.

Pressing my palms against the glass, my heart pounds in my chest. It thrums in my ears. When did it get painted over? How did I not notice it?

"What's wrong?" Naveed asks.

"You look like you saw a jinn," Kareem says.

"The wall. They painted over the mural."

"Huh." Naveed squints. "I guess you're right."

"There was a mural there?" Kareem says.

There *had* been a mural. It greeted me each morning when I woke up. It had graduation caps. And Bunsen burners.

And a telescope.

Seeing it was like a sign from the universe.

Was this what Mr. Adeel meant about art? The mural wasn't just a pretty painting. For whatever reason, it gave me hope. And now it's gone.

• • •

When the phone rings that evening, I'm so lost in algebraic equations, I nearly leap out of my skin. It's Amal. Seeing her number flash across the screen, I'm torn. It's almost lights-out, and I need to finish this problem. But

I picture Amal on the other line, her ear pressed to the phone, waiting for me to answer—

"Well, hello, stranger," Amal says when I pick up.

"Sorry," I tell her. "I've been meaning to call."

"I tried you a few times this week. So much for the daily calls you promised."

"Oh, Amal. I'm sorry." I wince. "It's so hectic here. The phone stays in my drawer most days."

"Relax, I'm kidding, Omar." She laughs. I hear the sounds of her little sisters arguing in the background. "Anyway, how's it going there? No issues or anything?"

"Issues? Nah. Everything's great." Knots form in my belly as the words leave my mouth. If she saw my expression, she'd see right through me. But we're twenty kilometers apart. My secret is safe with me. I scramble for something honest and true to tell her. "Kareem says everyone at his old school was snobby, but the kids here are mostly nice."

"That's great. And hey, we get to see you soon!"

"Four weeks and one day," I say. "Not that I'm counting."

"You forgot eighteen hours," she says. "Not that I'm counting either."

We talk for a little while longer. She updates me on her life. A trip to Lahore with her parents. The titles she picked up from Liberty Books. While she talks, I finish up my assignment. I'm trying my best to pay attention, but lights-out is in less than ten minutes.

"Uh-huh," I say again as she continues.

"Uh-huh?" she repeats.

"Sorry." I feel flustered. "The reception fades out sometimes. What'd you say again?"

Amal is silent. And then—

"I'll fill you in later. You seem busy."

"Yeah, it's almost lights-out. I'll talk to you soon, though," I say brightly before saying goodbye.

I feel guilty to be relieved to be off the call. But I'll see her soon enough. And by then, my grades will be better, and everything *will* be perfect. Amal's face will light up when I hand her the books I've already borrowed for her, and it'll make up for all the conversations we haven't been able to have. Nothing makes Amal happier than a pile of new books.

I glance at Kareem, and he looks back at me and nods. I don't have to say anything. He gets it. It's tiring pretending everything is great in front of everyone, but there's no point telling my mother or Amal. I'm the only one who can do anything about it.

Chapter 20

Not bad at all," my world history teacher says when he hands me back my test. I smile. A ninety-six! Now, *that's* an A! But biology brings even better news. So good, I almost don't believe it at first. But there it is, plain as day: 100 percent. A perfect score.

"I'm happy to report that everyone's grades are improving," Mr. Nawaz tells us. "As a reward, I've decided to give you a break. I'm dropping your lowest grade at the end of the semester."

"But what if you never got a bad grade?" a student sitting at the front asks. "Then what happens?"

"Then thank God for your genius brain and let the rest of us underlings catch that break, please," Kareem retorts.

The class erupts into laughter. When I look at Aiden, I can't believe it. Is he . . . smiling? Our eyes meet. He quickly looks away. But he smiled. He did. The first time I've seen it.

I trace the A on my page and smile, too. This was exactly what I needed. Could things actually be looking up?

• • •

But everything changes in English.

When Headmaster Moiz hands me back my *Othello* test, I knew it wouldn't be an A, but I'd read the book so many times I'd practically memorized it. I'd pored over the essay portion. Double-checked the grammar and spelling. I wasn't prepared for the D slashed in red across the top.

Blood rushes to my head. I stare at the page, willing the letter grade to change. Yes, the prompt was difficult. Yes, it took me all the way until the bell rang to finish. But a 68? A D? I've never seen that grade on a paper of mine. Ever.

"I must confess," Headmaster Moiz says, "I am surprised at the lack of improvement this far into the semester. Kareem did the best of the lot, but if you want to show you're truly Ghalib material, you'll all need to work harder than you ever have before."

He turns to the dry-erase board and writes our next assignment.

I grip the edge of my desk so tight, my hands grow numb. I feel Kareem's eyes on me, looking at me worriedly, but I don't meet his eyes. Afraid that if I do, I'll cry.

Work harder? I read textbooks while I eat my meals. I quiz myself on countries and capitals while I chop vegetables in the morning. I'm at the library more than I'm in my dorm.

How much more can I possibly do?

• • •

I head straight to the kitchen after art class.

Faisal is there. Kareem and Naveed, too. This kitchen has become my safe space. Looks like it's theirs, too. Naveed holds his test in his hands. His nose is red and his eyes are swollen behind his glasses. Basem and Shuaib are by the stove. They glance at us worriedly.

"How bad?" I ask him.

"Seventy-two. I can't believe it," he says shakily. "It's almost a D."

"You did better than me," I say. "I actually *did* get a D."

"I didn't even think the test was that hard," Naveed says in a tight voice. "How could we have done this badly? And

Moiz says we need to study harder. That's not humanly possible."

"That's the point," Faisal says.

"What do you mean?" I ask.

Faisal fixes his gaze down at the damp rag in his hand. "You haven't figured it out yet?" His easygoing demeanor is gone.

"Figured what out?" Naveed asks. He takes in Faisal's somber expression and then the cook's. He shrinks back. "You're—you're scaring me."

Faisal hesitates, but then—

"This is your weed-out year."

"'Weed-out year'?" I repeat. "What do you mean?"

"You know how if you have a garden, you have to constantly pull out the weeds so the garden looks fresh? For as long as I've been here, they make sure about half of the scholarship kids are gone after the first year."

"Hey, I'm no weed!" Kareem says. "My mother calls me her little turnip."

"It's not funny, Kareem," I say. "This means that with six scholarship students in our class . . . three of us will go?"

"Or all of you. I've seen that, too."

"That makes no sense," I protest. "Didn't our applications and grades prove we're not weeds? Why let us in if they want to let us go?"

"I bet it's because the school wants to look good," Kareem says. "They let us poor kids in. They seem great and generous. But they don't really mean it."

"Well, that's not gonna happen to us. We're not getting kicked out." I shake my head. "We'll study harder than anyone. We'll get our grades up. And yeah, I got a horrible grade today, but we're not *failing*."

"And Humza's grades are worse than ours," Naveed adds. "I was helping him with biology yesterday."

"Humza's not here on scholarship," Faisal says. "Scholarship students have to perform better than everyone else. You have to maintain an A-plus average."

Naveed stares at him. "But . . . catching up to an A-plus . . . that's almost impossible."

"Right," Faisal says.

None of us speak for a minute.

"Why do you think I'm the only Scholar in my final year?" he asks. "Look around. How many do you see beyond me in the upper years? There's Basit in eighth. Ali and Aamir are in the year behind me. There are hardly any of us."

I lean against the wall, feeling shaky. I know the earth is still spinning, but everything feels like it has ground to a halt. That's why Headmaster Moiz called Faisal the best scholarship student. Faisal wasn't only the best, he was one of the only ones.

"Should've known this was all too good to be true," Naveed whimpers. "To get into a place like this." His shoulders tremble. "We're doomed."

"Hey—hey." Kareem pats his back. "Take a deep breath in. Deep breath out. You'll be all right. We'll figure this out. It'll be okay."

Kareem's saying that to help Naveed keep it together. But will we really be okay?

"It's tough," Faisal says. "Year after year, seeing students like us coming in all excited but then having to leave before they can finish. I never know how to tell anyone how impossible it all is."

"I guess in a way it's good to be put out of your misery earlier rather than later," Basem says. "Better to know sooner than later that you'll be a ghost boy."

"Ghost boy?" Naveed looks up. "Wh-what's that?"

"Oh"—he hesitates—"it's what we call the kids who leave."

"Why? What happened to them?" Kareem asks.

"Never hear from most of them," Faisal says.

"I'm sure they're fine," Shuaib interjects. "Faisal, you remember Nauman, don't you? I ran into him a couple months back. He'd just enrolled at a local college. Whatever happens, you don't need this school to make it. You'll land on your feet."

He's wrong about that. This place *was* me landing on my feet. I think about the day I got the news of my acceptance to Ghalib Academy. I'd met Amal by the stream. When I told her, her eyes lit up like the sun. And when I told my mother, she hugged me so tight, I thought she'd never let go. At my going-away party, they said I carried with me the pride of my village.

My eyes fill with tears. What will everyone think of me if I go back to them a failure? How could this school bring us here when they never planned to keep us?

I think of the boys who came before me. Who walked these halls with hopes and dreams as wide as the blue sky outside. And one by one they've left—only to become whispers of memories—like Basem said, ghosts. Wiped clean like the mural. Like they never existed.

Naveed—and now Kareem, too—look as devastated as I feel. But as the shock wears off, anger replaces it.

"We'll prove him wrong," I say. "Midterms are in three weeks. They count for twenty percent of our semester grade. We'll ace them. And then next semester, our grades will be so good, our teachers will be shocked."

"Got plans to steal answer keys?" Kareem mutters. "Because otherwise there's no chance."

"There's a chance," I say. "There's definitely a chance. Kareem, you're doing better than the rest of us in English. My best subject is math. And Naveed, you have an A average in biology, don't you?"

Naveed wipes away tears with his shirtsleeve and nods.

"There you go," Kareem says. "Add us up and you get yourself one perfect student."

"We'll help each other. We've been studying hard. Now we'll study smarter. We're going to prove them wrong."

Kareem and Naveed look doubtful. The truth is, I'm not so sure either. But I think of Headmaster Moiz's smug face.

We *will* prove him wrong.

Chapter 21

Come on, guys, how can you say no to soccer again?"
Humza's standing with Marwan at the entrance of my
dorm room. A soccer ball's tucked under his arm.

"Yeah, it's Friday!" Marwan exclaims. "And this week's
movie night."

I glance at Kareem; I see the longing on his face.

"Sorry. But . . . we have to catch up," I tell them. As much
as I hate not being able to play soccer, I hate disappointing
them even more.

"You know some of us manage to study *and* have a life,
right?" Marwan says. "It's not like the rest of us don't have
the same classes you do."

"Exactly. You're not robots," Humza adds.

"I *wish* we were robots," Kareem says. "Then we could code everything we need into our brain."

"Next week," I tell them. "Maybe we'll be caught up by then."

"Forget the number one nerds club." Marwan huffs. "They're no fun anymore."

I watch them walk away. Marwan acts like we think being stuck in a room on a Friday night instead of having fun is what we *want* to do. He doesn't get it. Because he can't.

An hour later, the sounds from the movie playing outside echoes into our room. It vibrates the window.

"I definitely need to get earplugs," Kareem says glumly.

Our door creaks open, and Naveed steps inside with the biology textbook tucked under his arm. He sits on my bed and props it open. We get to work, dividing the vocabulary words into thirds and writing up flash cards to quiz each other with after.

"Is that your art project?" Naveed points to the collage resting on top of my dresser.

"Yeah, thought I'd get an early start."

"You used newspaper on it?" He squints.

"Yep," I tell him. "I'm making a collage. It'll be part of the solar system eventually."

I've been reading more about Shehzil Malik. Her art's been on posters, murals, and even clothing. In one article, she said when things are hard, that's when you have to be stubbornly optimistic. I look at the three of us right now: pens in hands, jotting down the definitions of *larvae* and *pupae*. That's us right now. Stubborn. And hoping as hard as we can that we'll make it through.

Music starts blaring from Aiden's room next door.

"Great. Concert time." Kareem flings his flash cards onto the floor. "Anyone want to peek over to see if he's break-dancing in there?"

"I'll leave that to you, little turnip," I retort.

"Hey!" Kareem tosses a pillow at my head. "Only my mom's allowed to call me that!"

"What do you think the headmaster will say when our grades suddenly improve? Think he'll get suspicious that something is up?" Naveed asks nervously.

"He'll probably launch a full investigation complete with undercover detectives and everything. Declare it a big conspiracy," Kareem says.

"It *is* a conspiracy," I say. "We're studying more than anyone in the history of the universe."

"Well, the number one nerds club's gotta live up to its reputation, after all!" Kareem says.

Chapter 22

Volleyball is officially my least favorite sport," I say as Coach Zulfi blows the whistle signaling the end of class. My wrist and hands are pink and sore from the force of slamming the ball.

"Once you get the hang of it, it's fun," Humza says. "It's all about getting the hand positioning right."

"But it's way better to play it at the beach," Marwan adds. "I'm going to Barcelona with my parents for winter break, and there's this stretch of beach where there's just net after net."

"We're going to Spain, too! But Granada. Again." Humza rolls his eyes. "My mom's obsessed with the Alhambra. But she promised we'll take the ferry to Morocco this time."

I listen to them trade stories about gross airplane food and hotels with bad Wi-Fi. We're all seventh years who love soccer and hate oatmeal. But at moments like these, I remember yet again how different we are.

"What about you, Omar?" Marwan asks me. "Heading anyplace fun for winter break?"

At moments like these, I realize, they forget I am different from them, too.

"Nah, just going home," I tell him.

"Aw, too bad," Marwan says sympathetically. "But hey, over the summer, maybe you could come with me to Indonesia," he adds. "My parents have a house on the beach. We can go snorkeling!"

How many homes does Marwan's family have? Technically, I don't even have one. My mother and I fashioned a living space from a shed. If Marwan saw where I lived, he'd probably pity me. But nobody should feel sorry for me. I *can't wait* to go home. To eat my mom's cooking and spend time with my friends. There's no place else I'd rather be.

When the bell rings, everyone heads toward the gym. I'm moving to join them when Coach Zulfi calls out to me.

"Omar?" He waves to me. "A quick word?"

I jog over. I know volleyball was harder for me than the other sports we've learned, but I couldn't have been so bad as to deserve a private reprimand?

"Haven't seen you on the soccer field with your friends lately. Everything okay?"

"Oh. Yes, Coach. I miss playing, but it's just that I have so much studying to catch up on."

"I admire your work ethic," he says. "But you should keep up the scrimmaging. And try to come to a game or two. You can even warm the bench and get up close and personal."

"Really?"

"Our next game is here at Ghalib. I know it'll pull you from studying for a little while, but I think it'll be good to know what to expect once you're on the team." He pats my shoulder. "Next year, you'll be a shoo-in."

A shoo-in. Coach said I would definitely make the team. He wants me to warm the bench at the next game.

His words should make my heart soar. But in order for there to even be a next year, I have to get the grades to get through this one.

Chapter 23

I'm done." Kareem groans and falls backward onto the bed. "I know you said brains can't actually break from too much studying, but my brain's about to prove you wrong."

I yawn. It's ten past midnight. Naveed, Kareem, and I have been up studying for hours huddled by the desk lamp in our room. A folded blanket lines the gap beneath the door.

"I'm tapped out, too," I say.

"But it's working," Naveed says. "I got a ninety-nine in history. I couldn't believe it! I think Mr. Khalid couldn't believe it either."

"I got a ninety-six. I'll catch up to you next time," I tease.

"You can try. But not everyone can be as good as me."
He grins.

"Hey!" I raise my eyebrows. "You're starting to sound
like Kareem."

"I'll take that as a compliment." Kareem laughs.

There's a sharp rap on the door.

The three of us sit up.

"What's going on in there?" someone says on the other
side.

Slowly, I walk to the door and open it.

"Mr. Nawaz?" I say. Without his glasses, it's hard to recognize him. And instead of wearing his usual button-down
shirt tucked into khakis, he's in pajamas and a pale robe.

"Filling in for the warden today. Omar, what are you
doing up so late?" He peers over my shoulder. "What are *all*
of you doing up? It's past midnight."

My stomach churns. He's a nice enough teacher. He's
even dropping our worst biology grade. But at the end
of the day, he is a teacher. And we are in violation of the
rules.

"We're sorry," I say quickly. "We were catching up on
our homework."

"You were *studying*?" He looks at the open books on
the floor.

"It's just that with midterms," I say, "there aren't enough hours in the day to get everything done."

"Lights-out at nine o'clock is for a good reason. Sleep is important. It's as important as the work you do. Being up this late is a clear violation of the rules."

"We won't do it again," Kareem says.

"Yes. Promise." Naveed's lower lip trembles. His face is growing pale. "Please, sir. We're really sorry."

Mr. Nawaz studies us all quietly, and I feel my mouth go dry. But then he points a stern finger at us. "Don't violate the lights-out rules again, okay? Naveed, back to your room now."

• • •

"I was sure we were at least going to get detention," Kareem says once it's the two of us again.

"We got lucky."

"Definitely. I'll take him over my dad catching us anytime," Kareem says.

Aiden should never have taunted Kareem about his father, but I hope now that the truth is out there, Kareem can breathe a little easier. It's nice to hear him talk about his father.

"Do you ever wonder what all the hard work is for?" Kareem asks. "We study every second we're awake and don't have time for any fun these days. Is it going to be worth it?"

"I'm not sure," I admit. "It has to be, though, right? Once we're done here, we can do whatever we want to with our lives."

"I'm going to be a doctor," Kareem says. "Definitely a doctor. But not just any doctor."

He tells me about his little sister. She has an illness no one can name. Without a name, no one can cure it. Kareem wants to be a disease detective. He wants to help his sister.

I tell him my own dream of being an astronomer. I've never told anyone at this school before. When I say it, Kareem doesn't frown or act puzzled. Knowing me, he says, it makes perfect sense.

I smile as I drift off to sleep. Finding out how hard it was to actually stay at this school, I'd started pushing away my dreams, afraid it would hurt more if it all crashed down.

But maybe holding on to your dreams is how you make your way through.

Chapter 24

The dining hall buzzes with energy because today's the day we start our break. In a few hours, I'll get to see my mother, Amal, Fuad, and Zaki. The farm kitties!

"My father's picking me up right after school," Naveed tells us. "As soon as art class ends. I stuffed my duffel in my locker so I can run out as soon as the bell rings."

"Malik Uncle is picking me up around five o'clock," I tell him. "My mom's making bhindi. My favorite!"

"Yum. Make sure to eat some for me," Kareem says. "I'll be thinking of you all while I'm stuck here."

"Oh, Kareem." I wince. "Sorry." How could I have forgotten his father didn't get time off, and Kareem was staying here with him?

"It's fine." He shrugs. "I'll get a head start for next semester."

"What about your mom?" Naveed asks. "Couldn't you go see her?"

"We're three hours and two bus switches away. My dad doesn't think it's safe for me to go alone."

"That does sound scary." Naveed's eyes grow big. "I'd be afraid I'd get off at the wrong stop and get lost."

"I'll come back early," I tell him.

"Nah. It's fine. Really," Kareem says. "Summer will be here soon enough. And on the bright side, the gym will be all mine for days. I'll become the best three-point shooter this school's ever seen. Might even practice penalty shots with the soccer ball. Better watch out when you come back!"

"Good! I could use some competition." I grin.

"Now, *that's* trash talk!" Kareem exclaims, laughing. "You're on!"

Kareem swats my arm playfully. I'm glad he's got a good attitude about it, but it doesn't change the fact that it stinks to be at school while everyone else is away.

• • •

My head is in the clouds when we sit down in English class. I'm thinking that even Headmaster Moiz can't get to me, because in just a few hours, Malik Uncle will be here to take me home. But I'm proven wrong when he hands back our latest essays.

It's not my grade. I didn't fail or anything. I got a B-minus. One of my better grades in this class. But there's a yellow sticky note on it with four hastily scrawled words: *See me after school.*

I don't know what it's about, but there's no way it's anything good.

"Want me to come with you?" Kareem asks as we file out to the hallway after art class.

"It's okay," I tell him.

"Well, if you need me, I'll be in our room," Kareem says.

I walk down the hall, past our English classroom, and into the office area. My feet sink into the plush carpeting. A row of spotlights shines above the receptionist, who sits at the front desk, typing on the computer.

"Can I help you?" she asks brightly when I approach her.

"I—I need to see the headmaster," I say. "He wanted to meet me after school."

She checks a schedule on her table. "Omar, right? Last door down the hallway."

Portraits of former headmasters watch me as I make my way to the headmaster's door.

"Come in," he says when I knock.

A framed photo of him with his arms around two smiling boys rests on his desk, and certificates are displayed on the walls. Plants line the back windowsill, and curtains flutter from the breeze through a half-open window. I blink in surprise. I'm not sure what I was expecting, but it definitely wasn't this. Headmaster Moiz gestures to an empty seat across from him.

"I was heartened by your essay," he says when I sit down.

I smile upon hearing these unexpected words. The headmaster isn't smiling. But he's not glowering either.

"Considering where you were academically when the year began," he continues, "you're showing progress."

"Thank you, sir," I say with a rush of relief. "I hadn't done a lot of essay writing before Ghalib."

"I could tell," he says. "The more you practice, the better."

"I'm studying every chance I get," I told him. "And I—"

"Now, that's not really true, is it?"

He stares at me for a moment before speaking again.

"Coach Zulfi thinks you are an excellent soccer player. He's seen you on the soccer fields and says you've got enormous talent."

My cheeks grow warm. "Yes. But—"

"Playing on the fields isn't forbidden. But I am concerned by the choice, given how fragile your status here is. I've seen far too many students squander their opportunity. Games are fun. But the work is what will take you where you need to go. I suggest you use your break wisely. The stakes are high, and to make it through, you'll need to buckle down and focus. Understood?"

I manage to nod. I manage to stand. I manage to say goodbye.

He said I'm doing okay. This wasn't a threat.

So why does it feel like one?

Chapter 25

Malik Uncle pulls the motorcycle out of the parking lot, and we zoom past fields and farms as we head toward home. The wind that whips against my face as we speed down these gravel roads is cool. Almost chilly. I swallow the lump that's settled into my throat. I've been looking forward to going home since August. And now? I can't push the conversation with the headmaster out of my mind.

Malik Uncle slows as we approach our village. My breath catches when I see the produce stall, the post office, the pharmacy. People making their way home from the stores. It's like nothing has changed.

"Omar! Wait up!" a voice shouts.

It's Fuad! He's with Zaki. They break into a light jog behind the motorcycle and follow us until we pull up in front of Uncle's home. I look at Amal's front door. The narrow walkway to the right leads straight to my own place. I smile. I'm home.

"Too good to say hi to us?" Fuad says, hurrying up to me.

"What? No!" I say quickly. But Fuad is grinning. Zaki gives me a high five.

"That uniform is spiffy." Fuad whistles.

"Do you have to wear it every day?" Zaki says. "The tie's gotta be itchy, right?"

"So, is it true?" Fuad interrupts. "I heard Ghalib's gymnasium is *huge*! It's got four basketball courts, right?"

"Um . . ." I hesitate. "I guess it is a pretty big—"

"And do they really have *horses* at the school?" Zaki frowns.

"For polo," I say. "But I haven't even seen—"

"And the recreation room—" Fuad interjects.

"Yeah!" Zaki says to Fuad. "I saw pictures of it online. They have a TV that takes up half the wall."

"That's it. I'm applying next year." Fuad folds his arms. "I'll even wear that uniform!"

"Get real," Zaki scoffs. "They don't let just anyone in. You have to be a genius like Omar!"

"Oh." Heat floods my face. "I'm not—"

"Omar." Malik Uncle places a gentle hand on my shoulder. "We should probably get inside. Dinner is waiting. Everyone is excited to see you."

"Well, glad you're home!" Zaki thumps my back. "Come out tomorrow. We'll kick the ball around."

I promise I'll try, and as I follow Uncle into the house, I hear Fuad's fading voice as he walks away.

"He's so *lucky*."

Lucky. There's that word again.

If they only knew the truth.

. . .

"He's home!" Amal's younger sisters Safa and Rabia sing out as soon as I step into their house. They race toward me. Lubna, the baby, crawls over, looking up at me curiously. I smile and wave at her and take in the sofas in the drawing room. The beige walls. Amal's home is practically my own. I've grown up here. And in this moment, it feels like I've never left.

"Omar."

Amma! My mother stands by the entrance of the courtyard, her hand on the doorknob, her chador wrapped loosely around her head. So much of the village has stayed the same, but when she approaches me, she seems different. When I hug her, I realize the change isn't in her. It's me.

"Someone grew." She smiles.

I haven't been gone *that* long, have I? But the proof is right here. I'm as tall as her.

Her eyes brim with tears. My own eyes widen with concern.

"Don't worry," she says. "These are happy tears, I promise. So good to see you after so long."

"Omar! You're back!" Amal rushes out of her room.

We take a step toward each other before pausing. Our parents know we speak, but we are never allowed to be alone. And a hug? That's out of the question.

"Welcome home." She grins. "Bring any books for me?"

My stomach sinks. "Oh, no, Amal! I'm so sorry, I had a whole bunch of books for you and I forgot to bring them— my day got so busy—"

"I was only teasing," she says. But I know Amal well enough to notice how quickly she looks away. I've disappointed her. Of course I have.

My mother ushers us into the courtyard to eat. A shard of sadness pricks me. It seems like no matter where I am, I'm disappointing someone.

Chapter 26

Hope that rooster didn't wake you," my mother says from the other side of the curtain the next morning. "You should sleep in as late as you want to."

"I've been up studying for a while," I tell her. I don't mention that I tossed and turned most of the night because the pillow seemed thinner than I remembered, and the woven ropes of the charpay prickled my back.

She parts the curtain and smiles sleepily at me.

"Good. We're making a big breakfast. All your favorites. I'm going to check on the dough. I kneaded it last night."

"Anything I can do to help?" I ask as she slips on her sandals.

"You can feed the chickens. And set some milk out for

Banu and Shamu. You know those two cats skulked around our house after you left? They probably missed you."

"Those cats don't miss anyone," I say.

"I said they *probably* missed you." She laughs. "You always *were* the one who snuck them leftovers."

"I'll feed them. As soon as I finish this page," I promise.

"No time off during your break?"

"I'm trying to get ahead for the next semester."

"Make sure you set some time aside to relax, okay? It's not every day we get to spend time with you." She kisses the top of my head.

I push back the swell of sadness. I wish I could take her advice.

When I walk out to feed the cats, they hurry over as I set their saucers down. Shamu sidles up to me and purrs. But Banu backs away when I grow near. They're so big now!

"Banu." I squat and extend a hand. "It's me. Your buddy."

She flattens her ears and then takes off toward the sugarcane field.

She's forgotten me already.

• • •

The scrambled eggs are piping hot. The homemade butter sizzles on top of my paratha. My mouth waters. Everything at Ghalib is touted as gourmet, and Shuaib's cuisine is delicious, but there's nothing like my mother's home cooking.

"What's your favorite subject at school?" my mother asks.

"I like math," I say. "But art is growing on me, too."

"Art?" Amal asks. "Really?"

"I know." I laugh. "It surprised me, too. I'm making a collage for a project using magazines and newspapers. It's actually fun."

"Maybe you'll end up liking art, too," Uncle says to Amal.

"Art?" I look at her, puzzled. "They're teaching art at the local school?"

"No, but they have art classes at Iqra. Remember? I told you I applied when we last talked."

I flush. I knew I'd missed some things on our last call, but how could I miss *that*?

"Amal. That's incredible," I manage to say. "You'll definitely get in."

"I don't know about *definitely*," she says. "It's pretty selective."

"I'm sure Miss Sadia wrote a full-length novel about what a great student you are."

"Kind of." Amal blushes. But then her expression grows a bit more somber. "But it is expensive. We're waiting to see if they'll offer any kind of scholarship."

"The harvest was good this year," her father says. "We'll find a way to make it work."

I hope Iqra doesn't have the same scholarship rules as my school. But she wouldn't struggle like I am. Amal's an *actual* genius.

"By the way"—my mother turns to me—"how many clubs did you end up signing up for?"

"I'm guessing five," Amal says. "One for each day of the week. I'm right, aren't I?"

My smile fades. The steam from the chai resting at my feet rises in swirls.

"Wait. It's not *ten*, is it?" she exclaims. "You doubled up, didn't you? No wonder you're so busy."

"I . . . uh . . . I didn't sign up for any."

"Are you joking?" Amal's sugar spoon clatters onto the saucer.

"It's complicated. I didn't want to overload." I avoid her eyes. "It's a busy semester."

"Omar! You're going to pretend you didn't have a list of all the different clubs ranked in order from top priority to least? That was half the point of going!"

"Amal," her mother says.

"Maybe next year." I force a shrug.

The conversation veers to other topics, like the extra two acres of farmland Uncle bought while I was away, and the unexpectedly good harvest. I'm careful to avoid Amal's piercing gaze as the conversations wash over me. I try my best to focus. I want to be here with them and just *be*, but Moiz's disapproving face keeps flashing before my eyes. And the ghost boys—I can't become one of them.

Once the meal's over, I excuse myself to get back to work. As I step out the door, I hear it: the tapping of a spoon against a bowl. *Tap. Tap. Tap.* I pause mid-step. I know that signal well. Whether made with a bicycle horn or a knock against a window or a wall, those three notes are the code for Amal and me to meet by the stream.

A part of me longs to hurry over to our secret spot and see her. Catch up. But there's the other part of me, too, the part that knows she'll ask me how I am. How I *really* am. I can't tell her. I'm still burning with shame from Headmaster Moiz's rebuke. If I meet her alone, everything will tumble out of me.

I don't turn to meet Amal's gaze. I keep walking home.

She'll go to the stream. She'll sit on the fallen tree trunk. She'll wait.

I'll pretend I didn't hear those taps. I have a good reason.

Once this is all behind me, I'll explain everything to her. I just hope she'll understand.

Chapter 27

When I wake the next morning before the sun rises, I hurry to feed the chickens. One less thing for my mother to do. But when I reach the coop, I pause. Amal's next to it. Her arms folded. Before I can speak, she does.

"I waited for an hour, Omar. We haven't seen each other since August, and you stand me up?"

I study the ground.

"I bet you're up extra early to feed the chickens to avoid me, huh?"

"No." I shake my head. "That's not it."

"Did I . . . do something?"

"Of course not," I say quickly.

"Then what is it?" Her expression softens. "You know you can tell me anything."

I can't. I can't tell her this. And as much as she searches my face for an answer, I am not going to burden anyone else with this.

"Amal, I'm sorry I didn't meet you. It's just . . . I'm busy. I have so much work to catch up on."

The truth. I stick to the truth. Nothing I said to Amal was a lie.

"Seriously? You're home after months away and can't take a little bit of a break?"

"No. I can't." My words come out sharper than I mean them to.

"What's going on, Omar?" She takes a step closer. "It's like you don't care about us anymore."

"Sorry."

"You don't have to say sorry. Something's bothering you. I know it can't be easy there. Completely on your own."

"I'm not on my own. Kareem's there, too."

"Right. But you see him every single day," Amal says. "Now you're finally home and too busy for *us*."

"Listen. I'm sorry I didn't bring you some books. That I didn't do book club."

"What?" She stares at me.

"That's what you're really disappointed about, isn't it?"

"You think this is about books? Really?" Her voice cracks. "You've been gone for so long . . . I wanted to talk to you yesterday without worrying about who's listening in. I missed you, Omar."

"Well, maybe you should stop missing me so much, then," I blurt out. "Everyone needs to get used to the fact that I'm at Ghalib. My life is there now."

I regret the words as soon as they leave my mouth. But it's better she thinks I've changed than to know the truth: that I am failing her and everyone in this village, including myself.

Amal flinches like I've slapped her. She turns and walks away.

And as much as I want to, I don't call her back.

Chapter 28

My mother sits on a chair by our open door, letting out the hems on my uniform pants. Outside, I hear the sound of neighborhood kids playing a game of cricket on the street.

"At the rate you're growing, I'm wondering if we need to buy you some new clothes," my mother says.

"They weren't *that* short," I protest.

"Next year, I'm getting you a size up. We can always hem them in and then let them down as needed."

If there is a next year.

"Looks like it's almost time for dinner." She glances outside at the setting sun.

"Can I eat here?" I ask her. "I need to catch up on my math work."

"Again?" she says. "You ate separately yesterday, too."

I fix my eyes on the papers on my charpay. It's been one day since my confrontation with Amal, but our exchange runs in a loop in my mind. How could I have said what I did to her? Never in my life have I so much as raised my voice around her. I'd never seen her look at me like that. Would she hate me forever?

"Omar, what's wrong?" my mother says. "You're not my cheerful son anymore. If you don't tell me what the matter is, I'll only worry more. Is there a problem at school?"

"No." I shake my head. I can't tell her about school, but I have to tell her something . . .

"Amal and I had an argument," I finally say. "She wanted to talk. See how I was. And I don't know, I think I haven't been sleeping properly or something, and . . . I lost my temper."

"Why don't you do your special knock and go meet her? Then you can properly apologize."

"What?" I look up at her.

"Oh, come on." She chuckles a little. "You knew I knew, didn't you? Go on, talk to her. You're only here a short while. Don't leave behind any regrets."

. . .

I dig my feet into the dirt. I am standing next to the fallen tree behind the sugarcane field where we always meet. Green stalks tower a few yards away. I beeped my bike horn outside the window of her home. Three taps in quick succession. I saw her through the glass. She looked up from the sofa. She heard. But will she come?

I look at my phone. Twenty minutes. Twenty-one. Twenty-two. My heart sinks. She's not coming. And it's what I deserve.

Just then, the sugarcanes rustle on this windless morning. And then—Amal. Her arms folded, she walks toward me. Her expression is unreadable.

"I'm sorry." I rush toward her. The words stumble out of me. "I'm so sorry, Amal. For yelling at you. For what I said. I didn't mean it. You are the last person I'd ever want to hurt."

She studies me for a moment. Finally she says, "I'm worried about you."

And just like that, my shoulders slump. I didn't want to tell anyone, but here by the stream, with only Amal and the birds fluttering overhead, the words spill out of their own accord.

"It's hard at Ghalib. It's *so* hard. I'm falling behind and I have no clue how I'm going to hang on."

"Omar." She comes closer. "I'm so sorry. You always said things were fine . . ."

"I didn't want to bother you. Not like you can change any of this."

"But talking about it could help you feel better."

"It won't. Not in this situation."

"Try?"

And so I do. I tell her about the chores, the insurmountable amount of schoolwork. How my stomach hurts all the time. Even now. And I tell her the rest of it, too. The impossible scholarship requirements. How they leave me feeling like each day is a race I can never win.

When I finish, I feel a little dizzy. But my heart doesn't feel quite so heavy anymore.

"It sounds awful," she says.

"It's not all bad. My friends are really nice, so it could be worse."

"I know," she says. "It's okay to be thankful for some parts of it, but it's also okay to say some parts stink. I wish you'd told me."

"It's just . . . Ghalib is so hard to get into. I'm lucky to be there at all."

"You can be lucky. And it can still be hard. It can be both."

"The headmaster is the worst," I say. "He teaches English, and surprise, surprise, that's the subject I'm doing the worst in. I think he gets a kick out of picking my papers apart."

"Why don't you ask him for help?"

"Yeah, that would work," I scoff.

"I'm serious! Ask him to tutor you. Asif's always happy to give extra sessions to anyone who asks over at the literacy center."

"That's because Asif is a nice person," I remind Amal. "In my situation, it would be like walking into a bear's den and expecting a fuzzy hug."

"What's the worst that can happen?"

"He'll maul me to death?"

"Very funny."

"I'm telling you. He's a mean old bear."

"Well, even so, the worst that'll happen if you ask for his help is he'll say no."

"Amal . . ."

"Be brave, Omar."

"Asking a teacher for help isn't brave." I crinkle my nose.

"If it's hard to ask, and you're asking anyway, you're being brave. Promise you'll try?"

"I promise I'll think about it," I tell her.

• • •

And I do think about it. I think about her words the rest of my time at home. As I say goodbye to my mother. As I sit on Uncle's motorcycle and speed back toward Ghalib Academy.

I am not brave like Amal.

Not by a long shot.

But Amal believes in me. Which makes me believe a tiny bit in myself.

Chapter 29

Your project is really coming along," Mr. Adeel says to me after class. I'm working on my collage, cutting and pasting to get the background exactly right, and choosing the best paper scraps to make Pluto.

"The border idea was good," I tell him. "Now I need to make sure Pluto really stands out."

"What about painting Pluto?"

"Oh. I'm not good at painting."

"It's not as scary as you think." Mr. Adeel laughs. He retrieves a bottle and a brush from the supply shelf and hands it to me. "This is an iridescent white. It'll make Pluto shine. Try it. You can always collage over it if it doesn't work."

I smile. That *is* the beauty of collages. No harm in trying something new if you can have a do-over if it doesn't go as planned.

But turns out, Mr. Adeel is right. The paint slides smoothly on, and now Pluto's almost glowing!

"Whoa," I exclaim. "It looks great!"

"See? You're getting the hang of it," he says. "And how's this semester going? Getting the hang of that, too?"

"I guess so," I tell him. "I did pretty good on all my midterms . . ." My smile fades a little. We *did* do well, but it cost us a lot. Movie nights. Rec room hangouts. Soccer scrimmages. "It's just"—I look at him—"it's been harder than I thought it'd be to fake it until I make it."

"Fake it until you make it?"

"Like you said. On the first day of school."

"Ah." He puts his hands on his hips. "Yes, it's a saying. It means if you want to get to where you want to go, you should act like you're already on your way there until you are."

"But what if I never get *there*?"

"What is 'there' for you?"

I look at my collage and take a minute to answer.

"Things *have* gotten easier," I finally say. "But I definitely don't have a handle on everything. Feels like I'm always trying to catch up."

"I don't know if any of us ever get to a place where we have a handle on *everything*," he says. "There's always something new to learn or figure out or solve. That's how life works. We're all figuring it out as we go. But that's also kind of the fun. Look at this collage! You'd never made one before, and now you're almost done."

I nod. What he's saying feels right.

"I know it may not seem like it," he says gently. "But we're all kind of faking it until we make it. Don't focus so much on making it that you lose out on the fun along the way that makes life worth living."

Mr. Adeel's advice makes sense. I want to have fun along the way, but can I afford to?

•   •   •

"There he is. Hey, Omar!" Humza shouts as I walk past the rec room.

Marwan, Humza, and Jibril are over by the Ping-Pong table.

"You came right on time!" Jibril says. "Up for a quick game?"

I'm about to say no, but then I think of Mr. Adeel's words. Plus, it *is* Friday . . .

"Sure," I say.

"Wait. Really?" Marwan says. "The president of the nerd club is in?"

"And will be kicking your butt!" I retort as I grab a paddle.

"That's right!" Humza cheers. "Now prepare to get destroyed, Marwan!"

It's been weeks since I held a paddle in my hand. My eyes stay steady, fixed on the ball. We score a point. Then another. When it's my serve, I hit the ball so hard it bounces on the other side and ricochets off the ceiling. We're winning. By three points now. Humza does a victory dance. I should be having fun, but all I feel is guilty that I'm here at all. It's like no matter what I do, I can't win.

Chapter 30

Back in my room, I look at my latest essay. A C curved like the moon is scrawled on the top.

"I didn't do great either," Kareem says.

I know he's saying this to make me feel better, but among the three of us, English is hardest for me. The dark hole I can't outmaneuver. And I've got to figure it out if I stand a chance of staying here. Amal's advice rings in my head. *Talk to the headmaster. See if he'll help.* She might be right, but the thought of voluntarily going into his office makes my stomach turn.

I'm leaning over to sharpen my pencil when Aiden walks past our open room. "Hey." He nods to Kareem.

Kareem nods before Aiden moves on.

"Did I just hallucinate?" I ask, turning to Kareem.

"Yep. You're hallucinating, Omar."

"No. Seriously." I straighten. "Did I miss something?"

"Yeah, while you were home for winter break," Kareem explains, "Aiden was here, too."

I shake my head. "Wow. That's the worst. To be stuck here with *him*."

"That's what I thought at first, but . . ." Kareem pauses. "I'm as surprised as you, but we got to talking at dinner and . . ."

"And now you're *friends*!" I exclaim.

"I don't know how to explain it. He was different. He dropped his attitude. We even played some foosball. He's pretty good."

"I can't believe it. You're *really* friends now!"

"Sure. We're officially best friends. Going to get bracelets engraved with our names tomorrow." Kareem rolls his eyes at me. "C'mon, Omar, give me a break. You would've done the same if you were in my shoes."

"Hm, maybe." I think of how he called me a charity case. Laughed at me on the soccer field. Insulted Kareem's father!

"Actually, no," I tell Kareem. "I don't think I'd hang out with Aiden even if he was the only kid in the whole school."

Chapter 31

The next time a parent open house arrives, I'm prepared. I don't hang around the front entrance watching families gather. And I'm happy about one thing: Naveed's parents came. His smile was so bright this morning, and he practically bounced with each step. At least there's that.

"Made you a keema paratha," Shuaib says when Kareem and I walk into the dining hall midmorning. "Fresh off the griddle." He places the stuffed flatbread on our plates.

"Wait. Are these the *famous* parathas?" I ask him.

"Yep." He bows with a flourish. "Consider yourself as well-fed as any celebrity."

"Thanks," I say. "But why?"

"What can I say? I'm in a good mood." He shrugs. Then with a small smile he adds, "And you're good kids. Can't I do something nice once in a while?"

The paratha is warm, salty, and delicious. I know why Shuaib made it for us. He knows how hard days like this can be on us. But I don't feel sad today. I feel grateful.

. . .

"Ready for another exciting day?" Kareem asks when we settle into the library.

"Can't think of anything else I'd rather be doing."

"Except everything else?"

"Exactly."

We work into the afternoon, barely speaking to each other.

"My brain hurts," Kareem finally says, cradling his head in his hands. "I'm telling you, it's not big enough."

"Kareem, for the hundredth time, brains don't work like that!"

"Just you wait! I'm going to become a brain doctor to prove it to you. But seriously—" He leans back in his chair. "How about basketball. A quick game or two?"

"Fine." I surprise Kareem by agreeing. "Just a quick one." The truth is, I could use a break, too.

The gym is empty when we step in. Kareem heads to the metal cage filled with basketballs and grabs one.

"Catch!" he shouts, tossing it to me. His voice echoes through the room. I catch the ball square in my hands. But then Kareem's attention moves away from me toward the door.

It's Aiden.

His eyes lock on to mine. My body tenses. He might have been nice to Kareem when it was only the two of them around, but it doesn't mean he's morphed into a different person. Is he trying to intimidate us? Hoping we'll slink away under his gaze?

"Hey," Kareem says.

"We're allowed to be here," I interject. "It's not against the rules."

Aiden doesn't reply. I bounce the ball to Kareem. It strikes the ground, and the noise echoes against the walls. Aiden can stare us down if he wants. We're not going anywhere.

"I used to play."

I pause. Slowly, I turn to him.

"Long time ago." He stuffs his hands in his pants pockets. "Horse. That was one of my favorites."

"'Horse'?" I repeat.

"You take turns shooting the ball, and every time you miss, you add a letter to the word *horse*. The first one to *e* loses."

"Why *horse*?" Kareem asks.

"No idea." He smiles a little. "But it's fun."

Watching him walk toward the door, I think about what I said to him during the first parent open house. That his parents didn't care enough about him to come. I'd said the words in anger. I did it to strike at him the way he lashed at us, but I didn't know then how true my words might have been.

I glance at Kareem. He nods.

"You want to play with us?" I ask.

Pausing, Aiden looks at me. "Really?"

"You can show us how the game works," Kareem says.

Horse ends up being an easy enough game—fun, too. I lose the first round. Aiden's out second. Kareem wins each one.

"You're good," Aiden tells Kareem.

"Trade you basketball tips for your foosball secrets?" Kareem says.

"Not sure my foosball is at *this* level," Aiden responds.

"True," Kareem says seriously. "Not everyone can have the gift."

Aiden's eyebrows shoot up. Then he laughs.

I know Kareem said Aiden wasn't so bad, but this still feels strange.

• • •

We head over to the dining hall for a snack break a few hours later. It's off-hours, but working behind the scenes has its perks. Kareem and I know where everything's kept, so we grab the bread from a cabinet and the jam and milk from the fridge.

"Shuaib made this jam from scratch," Kareem says, taking the last bite of his toast. "He's got magic in his hands. I bet there's some dessert in the freezer. Want me to check?"

"I don't know." I hesitate. "We didn't study much after our afternoon session."

"I'll grab our biology flash cards," Kareem says. "You scrounge for dessert? I'd call that a perfect solution, wouldn't you?"

"My parents forgot about winter break," Aiden says once Kareem leaves. He looks down at his empty plate. "Kareem probably told you that already."

"I didn't know they forgot. I'm . . . sorry."

He shrugs like it doesn't matter. But it's clear from his face it does.

"When I called my mother to ask what time they were coming, it turned out they were on vacation in Dubai. They forgot to mark me on their calendar. I thought maybe they felt bad about it. And maybe they'd come this weekend to the parent open house to make up for it. Guess not."

I shift in my seat. "That day . . . what I said about your parents . . ."

"I don't care." He shrugs again. "Not the first time they've forgotten about me and won't be the last. I'm used to being alone."

"It's awful they didn't come. But . . . we got to play basketball today. At least you didn't have to be completely alone."

"I'm always alone," he says. "Do you know how many schools I've been to? Singapore, Sharjah, Connecticut, and Sydney. Now back here. My father gets transferred all the time. What's the point of getting to know people when I'll be gone again?"

"Because at least while you *are* here, your time can be easier." I think of Amal. How I foolishly shut her out because I didn't want to lean on anyone. "Being alone makes everything harder than it needs to be."

"Sorry about earlier," he says. "The things I said. I don't know . . . Kareem's got his father here . . . they see each other whenever they want to. And you . . . you're so lucky."

"Lucky?"

"I can hear you from my room," he says. "You talk to your mother a lot. When you call, she always answers."

Lucky. Aiden with all his high-end electronics and a father who paid to upgrade the gymnasium thinks I'm lucky. The last thing I ever feel is lucky. I'm the kid doing chores. Who can't do any of the fun after-school activities. Struggling to keep up with my classes.

But I think of my mother, and Amal, and my community back home. The orange jalebis to see me off. Shuaib, who made his signature parathas for me.

He's right. I *am* lucky.

"If I were you, I'd give the friendship thing a try," I tell him. "See if it fits."

Aiden doesn't say anything. But he smiles. And he doesn't say no.

Chapter 32

In art class, Marwan swirls his brush, trying to match the style of Frida Kahlo. Aiden attempts to make a hot-air balloon from cardboard. I watch Naveed repaint his canvas white for the third time.

Mr. Adeel approaches and peeks over my shoulder. "*Stubbornly Optimistic*," he says, reading the words I've pasted along the bottom of the canvas. "Nice title."

"Thanks," I say. "I think I'm almost done now. I added stars to the background—they're the exoplanets in our galaxy—and the brightness along the edges is all the possibilities we don't even know about."

"So remind me," he says. "Why did you decide to make Pluto the center of your piece?"

I look down at shimmery Pluto and smile. "I like that Pluto's stubborn," I tell him. "Scientists said it couldn't be a planet like the others because it was too small and can't knock out all the space junk that crosses its path like the other planets do without even having to try. But planet or no planet, it's still out there doing its thing. And when I found a quote from Shehzil Malik about being stubbornly optimistic, it made me think about how I'm trying to make it here at Ghalib, but also about Pluto. It just kind of fit."

Mr. Adeel cocks his head and studies my artwork. I wait for him to remind me Pluto isn't a person. It doesn't have feelings. It doesn't *actually* care what scientists on Earth call it.

"I love it," he says. "You captured the spirit of her work and connected it to yourself. Good job, Omar. That's what this is about."

• • •

The final bell of the day rings. Everyone disperses through the halls.

Heading to the library, I think of my conversation with Amal. I *really* don't want to ask the headmaster for help. But if I'm going to be stubbornly optimistic about my chances of staying here, I need to do everything possible.

The handle of the door to the main office is cool to the touch.

"How can I help you?" the receptionist asks once I'm at the imposing wooden counter.

"I wanted to make an appointment to see Headmaster Moiz—" I begin.

"Oh! Well, he may have time right now. I'll check," she says.

"R-right now?" I manage to give her my name and watch her disappear for a minute.

He won't want to see me. He barely wants to talk to me when I'm in his class.

But apparently he does.

My heart somersaults as I step into his office.

"Mr. Ali, have a seat." He gestures to the leather chair across from him.

Gingerly, I sit down. His hands are folded on the desk.

"This is a surprise," he says. "I often summon students, but rarely do they arrive unannounced."

"I wanted to talk about my grades." I get the words out quickly. Before my courage leaves me. "I've gotten a handle on every subject but English. Grammar is tricky. And essays . . . they're impossible. I was hoping maybe . . . if it's okay . . . maybe you could help me see what I'm doing wrong?"

Butterflies flutter in my stomach as the silence stretches. Is he trying to figure out how to tell me I am a hopeless case? That no amount of studying can help someone like me?

"Essays are hard for many people," he finally says. "And grammar isn't the easiest."

"It's *so* hard! Sometimes you add an *es* after the *s*. Sometimes you don't. Some words like *fish* don't have anything at all to make them plural. I can't figure it out."

"I can help you."

For a split second I think I imagined he said it.

"Meet me here tomorrow. Same time. Bring your textbook. Let's figure out where you're getting stuck."

I asked for help.

He said yes.

Had it really been this easy?

Chapter 33

Headmaster Moiz explains essays to me after school. Today's our fourth tutoring session. He's not exactly a jalebi dipped in honey, but as he leans over and fixes my essay, he seems not quite as terrifying.

"You've done book reports at your old school, haven't you?" he asks me.

"Lots of them."

"I could tell, because that's what you kept trying to do with your essays. Summarize. That's what the quizzes are for. Essays are where you dive deeper and support what you're saying about the text."

"So, give examples for the points I'm making?"

"Exactly!" He smiles.

I know Faisal said we are weeds at this school, but I don't feel like a weed right now. It almost feels like Headmaster Moiz hopes I'll make it through.

"English is like any other language in the world," he says. "It feels intimidating because it's not the one you grew up with."

"But it has so many rules and exceptions."

"There are quite a lot," he agrees. "But once you know them, it's second nature. My own son found it perplexing as well when I walked him through it many a moon ago." He looks at the framed photograph of two boys I'd seen last time I was in his office. "Helped his own children figure it out as well."

I look at the picture. There's a home in the backdrop. The two kids look up at Headmaster Moiz with huge grins. I wonder if his son's the one taking the photograph. It's hard to imagine Headmaster Moiz having a son. And grandsons. A whole life outside of Ghalib. To me, it's felt like he arrived fully formed as a somber headmaster rooted right here in the halls of this building. But of course that's not true. Like me, his story goes beyond this place.

• • •

I spend the rest of the week working on what Headmaster Moiz taught me. By the third week, even though I can't explain exactly *how* it happens, something clicks. It's like how I once looked at the email system and saw only strange symbols, or at Picasso's art and saw only floating noses. I now see the assignments how I'm supposed to. Everything fits like the pieces of a puzzle. And it doesn't feel as scary anymore.

When he hands me back my next paper on Friday of that week, my stomach flips. It's a 90 percent. An A. Barely. But it's the first time I've seen that letter in this class.

I look up at Headmaster Moiz. He smiles at me before heading to the whiteboard to write our assignment for the next Monday.

I trace my finger over the grade.

It's happening. I've finally learned the secret language of this school. I'm finally turning things around. I only wish I'd asked him for help sooner.

Chapter 34

There's a knock on our door.

"Come in," I call out. Aiden opens the door. He settles down on my bed. I'm still getting used to this new Aiden.

"Cool art project," he says, pointing to my collage on the desk.

"He's a regular Picasso," Kareem chimes in from his desk.

"Well, Picasso." Aiden grins. "It's going to rain all weekend. Quick game of soccer while we can?"

"I'm in." Kareem rises.

I look wistfully out the window. I haven't set foot on the soccer field since last semester. My grades *have* been improving. I even got an A in English! And didn't Mr. Adeel say not to forget to enjoy the little things along the way? If getting an A in *English* isn't a reason to celebrate for a little while, what is?

We head onto the grassy field. I set the soccer ball on the ground. We take turns doing penalty shots. A little while later, Humza and Marwan join, too. The breeze makes the trees sweep and dance as we play, like they're a silent audience cheering us on. I check my watch when we finish. We played longer than I'd planned to, but it was worth it.

As we are leaving, I see Faisal with a group of kids coming onto the field wearing smocks.

"I'll catch up with you all in a second," I tell my friends.

"Hey," Faisal says when I jog up to him. He lifts a stick with a foam roller on the end.

"What are you guys doing?" I ask.

"Prepping the wall for the next mural."

"A new mural?"

"The old one was starting to look pretty messy, with paint peeling and all."

"What'll the new mural be?"

"Not sure yet," he says. "There's a contest going on among the upperclassmen to pick."

"Can I help?" I blurt out.

"Sure," Faisal says. "Grab a smock. Happy to have an extra hand."

I tie a smock on and grab a paint roller. Sliding the roller up and down, turning the wall a solid shade of white, winds up being satisfying work. The old mural might be gone, but something new—maybe better—is coming in its place. When we finish, my arms ache, but my heart feels full.

. . .

That evening, I speak to Amal. She tells me she heard back from Iqra. She's been wait-listed at the school, but she's first on the list and is hopeful it will work out. When she asks how I'm doing, I tell her about soccer and the mural.

"But I haven't told you the best part about my day yet," I tell her. "I got a ninety. In English."

I pull the phone from my ear as she lets out a yelp.

"Didn't I tell you?" she shouts into the phone.

"You did. This is thanks to you, Amal."

"Thanks to me? No. *You* did it. You asked him. You did the work. You got that grade."

I look at the paper and smile. Being brave paid off after all.

Chapter 35

've been meaning to talk to you about your artwork,"
Mr. Adeel tells me when the bell rings at the end of the day.
He walks over to me and picks up my collage and studies it.

"Of course," I say quickly. I look down at the collage.
"I'll do whatever I can to fix it up."

"No. Nothing like that. I was wondering if you would be
okay with my adding this piece to the Hall of Fame board
after your presentation."

"*My* art?" I stare at him.

"Yes." He laughs. "Can you believe I don't have a single
collage on the wall? Yours would be a mighty fine one to
add to the collection."

"But . . . I didn't even copy Shehzil Malik's work or even come close to it."

"That's right. This piece represents *you*, inspired by her. And I have to say Pluto's looking very stubbornly optimistic."

I study my canvas. He's right. Pluto looks pretty great. So maybe I really am a bit of an artist.

• • •

I swing by the computer lab on my way back to my room. I click through my emails. The student newsletter. The rain date for movie night. I pause at the next message. It's from our guidance counselor, Mrs. Rashid. But it's not her usual questionnaire. This email is two sentences long and is flagged *Important*. She wants to meet. Today, at four o'clock. I glance at the time. It's 3:55 p.m.

I hurry into the administrative wing and check in with the receptionist.

"She's with another student, but she's almost ready for you," the woman says. "Third door to the left. Just wait outside."

I've passed this door many times. Moiz's office is right down the hall. This is the first time she's asked to meet in person. As I approach it, Naveed parts the guidance counselor's door and steps out.

"Hey, Naveed," I say.

"Gotta run," he mumbles.

The year's ending soon, so Mrs. Rashid must be opting for in-person catch-ups instead. It makes sense.

"Omar, welcome," she says. "Please, have a seat."

I remember her from the first day I arrived, when she gave me my registration folder. She has the same red glasses. She opens a cabinet and pulls out a file.

"So tell me, Omar." She uncaps a pen and writes something in the folder. "As the year winds down, how has your time been here?"

I'm tempted to do what I've done since I've arrived—sugarcoat it. Fake it. But she really seems interested.

"It started off difficult," I admit. "But it's gotten better."

"Difficult?" She raises her eyebrows. "You always said everything was going great."

"I just . . . I didn't want anyone to think I was struggling. That I didn't belong."

"Omar." She sighs. "That's what I'm here for. At least part of why I'm here, anyhow. To help people navigate these sorts of things."

She jots something down. Before I can wonder what, she looks back up.

"The reason I invited you here is we need to discuss your grades," she says. "I got the latest update from your teachers, and you've had an impressive semester. From a nearly failing grade in English to getting straight As across the board. Your teachers speak very highly of you."

I smile. I worked so hard. Until my hands ached and my eyes blurred. But it's been worth it.

"Which is why what I have to say now brings me no pleasure." She leans forward, her elbows resting on the table. "I've been reviewing your grades—and where they need to be—and unfortunately, when we average in last semester with this semester, it simply won't be enough."

"Enough for what?" I ask.

"Enough to keep your scholarship, I'm sorry to say."

I stare at her. No. I misheard her. I must have.

"B-but I brought my grades up. You said the teachers are happy with me."

"You did. They are," she agrees. "But you're still going to be short of the requirement. It's close, but not close enough, I'm afraid."

"But—but—the school year isn't over yet," I stammer. "We still have finals. Mr. Nawaz is dropping the worst grade again this semester. I can bring my average up."

"Unfortunately, even if you got a perfect score on every final, your first semester is still going to bring you down."

My hands grow numb. My body feels like it's been dipped in ice water. I think of Naveed. He ran out of this room before I entered. Is he getting kicked out, too? Is Kareem?

"Please." My voice cracks. "You have no idea how hard we've been working. It's not fair."

"I know you're a bright boy. Your improvement is commendable. I've never seen anything quite like it. But these are the rules here."

She sighs like it's all weighing on her more than on me.

"You can stay until the end of the semester," she continues. "We want you to finish up and get your final grades; you can use them to apply elsewhere."

Elsewhere. I want to laugh, but it hurts too much. The counselor looks at me sympathetically. But how sympathetic can she be? I'm not the first boy who's sat across from her. I won't be the last.

Tears prick my eyes. I'm becoming a ghost boy after all.

Chapter 36

Naveed's alone when I push open his door. He looks at my face. "You too, huh?" he says in a dull voice.

I nod, unable to speak.

"Ami and Abu were so proud of me when they came for open house." His lower lip quivers. "This is going to break their hearts." Tears trail down his cheeks. "I kept telling myself it would be okay. Maheen always says to believe in yourself, and things will work out, but obviously it was stupid advice. She was wrong."

I want to comfort him, but what can I say? He's right. This is the end. Of everything. This is the asteroid crashing down on the dinosaurs. Nothing I say or do will make any of this better.

Could we have studied harder? I wonder. I really don't think so . . .

"There you are!" Kareem bursts into the room. "What are you both doing? Meditating?"

Neither of us speak.

"Whoa." He settles down across from us. "What's wrong?"

He doesn't know. Which means he didn't get an invite from Mrs. Rashid. At least one of us is safe.

"We were summoned to the guidance counselor's office this afternoon," I tell him.

"How come?"

"We're getting kicked out," I say.

"What?" Kareem startles. "Come on, Omar. That's not funny."

"No," Naveed says. "Not funny at all."

"They made a mistake . . ." Kareem's face pales. "They had to. We've worked so hard. All of us. And we're doing great now."

"Not great enough," I say.

"No." Kareem stands up, and the chair scrapes against the floor. "They can't do that. They can't."

"You know they can," I tell him. "And they are. Unless we can pay our way, we've hit the end of the road."

"There's gotta be another option," Kareem says. His voice rises. "We have to figure it out, that's all, and—"

"Stop," I say. My voice is louder than I intended. "It's over, Kareem. We tried. We failed. Sometimes kids like us succeed. Sometimes we go home."

He moves to speak, but I put up my hand. I don't want him to try and make us feel better. Try to say that there's a way out. A silver lining. Because there is none. The sky has fallen and it's landed squarely on my head. There's nothing and no one that can fix this.

Chapter 37

M r. Adeel flips the lights off. The classroom goes dark.

"Omar was brave enough to be the first presenter," he tells the class. "As a reminder, we're going through multiple presentations per class to stay on track, so please stick to the ten-minute limit. Now, without further ado, our first PowerPoint presentation." Mr. Adeel bows with a flourish before he walks to the back wall and settles down on a stool.

The light glows bright from the machine when I approach it. I pick up the clicker and look at the first image: Shehzil Malik at her laptop glancing back at us with a smile.

I launch into my rehearsed speech. "So many artists we learn about are from other places. Or they lived in different time periods. But Shehzil Malik was born and raised in Lahore." I click through the photos. "She uses different mediums, like clothing, murals, and graphic design, but no matter what, you can tell it's her by what she's saying."

What she's saying. A wave of grief washes over me.

She says not to give up.

She says to keep on trying.

She says to keep on hoping even when it's hard to hope.

But is that really the best advice?

"What *is* she saying with her work?" Mr. Adeel prompts me.

"She talks about justice," I say. "Resistance. She was one of the artists behind the Women's March in Islamabad." I flash through a mural she created, slides of people holding up posters for equality and justice for all.

"I remember that," a kid interrupts. "It was on the news."

"Thousands of people come from all over," Mr. Adeel says. "I went the first year."

I share my favorite works of hers, and then the presentation portion is done. I need to turn on the lights and talk about my art piece. I need to hold it up. Tell them what I've created. Explain my personal connection. The statement I'm trying to make.

I look down at the starry sky. Pluto shining bright. The words below: *Stubbornly Optimistic.*

I swallow.

"I chose this for the title." I clear my throat. "Because . . ." But the words won't come out. What had being stubbornly optimistic gotten me? Sleepless nights and fear and worry. Missed soccer games. I sacrificed the time I had at home with my family and friends over winter break trying to study. And even after all that, Ghalib is showing me the door.

"Earth to Omar." A paper ball grazes my elbow. It's Humza. He grins at me. There's a burst of laughter.

I just need to say a few more sentences. Then I'm done. But I'm not sure what to say. None of it feels true anymore.

"Omar?" Mr. Adeel walks toward me. "Everything okay?"

"No . . . everything isn't okay." My voice cracks. "I'm getting kicked out of school."

There's a collective gasp.

"Me too," Naveed says.

"Kicked out?" Marwan repeats.

"What're you talking about?" Aiden asks.

"What'd you guys do?" asks a kid in the front. "Steal an answer key?"

A bunch of students laugh at this.

"We don't have an A-plus average, and that was the requirement to keep our scholarships."

The laughter fades.

"A-plus? That's ridiculous!" Humza frowns.

"Yeah." Aiden gets up. "That's almost impossible."

"It is."

"I bet they're trying to psych you out," Marwan scoffs. "You know, so you do extra well on your finals or something. You're the nerdiest kids on campus."

"We were only the 'nerdiest,' Marwan, because we *had* to be," I tell him.

"Yeah. And finals won't make a difference," Naveed says.

"They made a mistake," Aiden says. "Your grades are way better than mine."

"My grades are kind of bad actually." Humza frowns. "No one had a talk with me."

"Doesn't work that way," Kareem says. "We have to do better because we're on scholarship. That's why we've been burying ourselves in work."

"He's right," Mr. Adeel says. I've never seen him so serious. "The scholarship requirements . . . they're ridiculous. I've seen too many bright and wonderful children come and go. I'm so sorry, Naveed and Omar."

"I . . . I had no idea," Marwan says.

"It's not fair." Aiden is getting flushed.

"Talk to Mrs. Rashid," Marwan says. "Or the headmaster. They've gotta listen to you."

"Let us know if we can do anything," another calls out.

"Yeah. Don't give up," Humza chimes in. "Isn't that what you said in the presentation?"

It's easy for them to say all this. Like I can convince this place to change when none of the kids who came before me could. I'd tried *so* hard. I'd even almost convinced myself that maybe, just maybe, Faisal was wrong about us being weeds. Because whenever I worked with Headmaster Moiz, he'd always seemed to be rooting for me.

I was wrong.

"We might go to the same school, but the rules are completely different for us," I say. "While you're practicing archery and playing chess, we have to sweep the cafeteria and chop vegetables. While you get to eat popcorn, we study flash cards. We might be *in* the same classes, but we're *from* different classes. Ghalib Academy wants to make sure we never forget."

Chapter 38

Lights-out was hours ago, but Naveed, Kareem, and I are still sitting on the floor between the two twin beds, with only a dim light between us. If the warden finds us now, it doesn't much matter that we're outside of curfew. Not for Naveed and me, anyway.

"A part of me's still stressed about finals." Naveed sniffles and wipes his nose with his sleeve. "But what's the point in studying?"

"It's wrong," Kareem says in a shaky voice. "How can I stay here when you both have to leave?"

"At least one of us gets to stay."

"I don't want to be here without you guys."

There's a knock on the door. It creaks open. But it's not the warden or Mr. Nawaz. It's Aiden. He slides down next to Kareem, facing me and Naveed.

"I read my whole acceptance form just now," he says. "There's nothing about a grade-point average we have to keep."

"Because your dad pays full tuition," Kareem reminds him.

"We can't let them do this," Aiden says. "We *gotta* come up with something. We can't just give up."

"Sometimes you have to know when it's too . . ."

My voice trails off as my eyes land on the collage resting on my desk:

Stubbornly Optimistic.

Looking at those words right now, something inside me shifts. I've memorized provinces and countries and capitals. I even asked Moiz for help. But . . . is it remotely possible I haven't been stubborn enough? Could we be so *stubborn* we didn't care if they told us it was time to go? Could we just refuse to take no for an answer?

"Your presentation was good . . . considering," Naveed says, looking over at the collage. "I'm not doing mine. I was already stressed about standing in front of the class like that. At least I can skip it now."

"It's not that . . ." I pick up the collage. "I'm thinking,

Shehzil's art is about resisting injustice. And what's happening to us *is* an injustice. What if we don't *let* them kick us out?"

"They probably have people to escort us off campus if we refuse to leave," Naveed says.

"I know!" Aiden's eyes light up. "I'll get my dad to give the headmaster a call. I'm sure I could guilt him into doing this for me since he never visited."

"Yeah . . . maybe," I say. I appreciate his offer, but I remember his father and how he stormed past us. I don't want to rely on him.

"I could write something," I say slowly. "A letter? Maybe the headmaster needs to hear from the students being affected why this is wrong. We can ask him to reconsider."

"I could write one, too," Naveed says.

"You really think he'd listen to your letters?" Kareem asks. "Not to be negative, but I'm sure other kids in the last fifty years have begged for this school to reconsider."

"Marwan and Humza said they'd help if they could," Aiden says. "How about you write the letter and we get everyone to sign it. You know, a petition."

"A petition." I look at Naveed. "You think?"

"We can try?" Naveed says. "What's the worst that can happen?"

He's right. The worst is already happening.

• • •

I stay up all night writing and then rewriting the words I will attach to the petition. These will be the most important words I will ever write. They need to convince Headmaster Moiz that putting higher expectations on scholarship students is unfair. That the school needs to stop treating us like second-class citizens.

Birds chirp outside my window by the time I'm done. My eyes feel scratchy. My head hurts. I staple blank pages to the back for the signatures that I hope will come. Looking down at my words, I hope they are enough.

Chapter 39

You really think people will sign this?" Naveed asks as we near the dining hall.

"Sure," Aiden says. "Lots of kids offered to help. I bet plenty of them will add their names."

I clutch the petition tightly in my hand and glance at Naveed. I'm nervous, too. Sure, people offered. But it's one thing to offer help. Another to actually follow through. Will anyone *really* put their name to this?

My doubts disappear when we enter the cafeteria. It's packed. Every seat is taken and students stand along the back of the wall. I recognize some other scholarship students. Faisal and some older kids. I've never seen it this busy for breakfast before.

Upon seeing us, everyone falls silent. Before I can say anything, Marwan speaks.

"What took you so long? We've been waiting forever!"

"Waiting?" I stare at them. "For us?"

"Yeah," Jibril says. "After everything you said the other day. About them expelling you . . . It's not right!"

Other kids murmur in agreement.

"We wanted to come up with a plan. To help," Humza says. "We can't do nothing."

They're here because of Naveed? Me?

"Well, to start, I wrote a petition to our headmaster asking him to reconsider the rules." I hold up the note with the stapled pages. "I was hoping you could add your names in support."

"I'll sign it," Aiden says. He grabs a pen and leans the paper against the table and writes his name.

The paper flies from table to table. They're signing it! Between Aiden's father calling and this, maybe we can do it. But before I can get too hopeful, Faisal clears his throat.

"I'm sorry to be the one to say it, but there's a petition every year about this. Doesn't mean it won't work *this* time," Faisal says. "But . . ."

His voice trails off, and I feel foolish. Why would Moiz care about signatures from a bunch of kids?

Aiden slams his hand against the table. "This is ridiculous!"

All eyes turn to him. Aiden straightens. "I'm asking my dad to pressure the school board. Maybe we could all ask our parents?"

"Sure," says Marwan. "I'll text my parents right now."

"That might not be enough." Humza shakes his head.

"*We* should do something, too," Aiden agrees. "Something they can't ignore."

"What do you have in mind?" Kareem asks.

"Don't know," Aiden says. "But there's so many of us here. We've got to be able to come up with something."

So many of us.

I look at everyone sitting here right now. The energy in the room is electric. That's it. That's the answer.

"The Women's March," I burst out. Everyone looks at me. "I told some of you about it in art class," I say. "Lots and lots of people protested with signs and banners. Thousands of people. It made the news because no one could ignore it."

"A walkout!" Humza brightens. "*That's* what we should do. There was this one movie where everyone got up and left their classrooms at the same exact time to protest. It was huge."

"It's not only in the movies," Marwan says. "It happens in real life, too. You pick a time and a day and everyone steps out at the same exact time to send a message."

"If all of us did it, they'd *definitely* pay attention," Aiden says.

"Maybe." I hesitate. "But it could also get you all in a lot of trouble."

"We don't want anyone else getting expelled because of us," Naveed says.

"We wouldn't. Not if all of us did it," Aiden says.

"Yeah, how can they kick *all of us* out?" Humza says.

"What do you think?" Aiden asks everyone. "This only works if everyone agrees to do it. Who's in?"

Kids exchange glances and whisper quietly. Some look worried. I don't blame them. I don't even know some of the people here. But then—

"I'll do it," says Humza.

"I'm in, too," says Faisal.

"Me too." Marwan raises his hand.

"Same here," says another.

"Show of hands," Aiden says.

And then—to my disbelief—everyone raises their hands.

"I'll talk to the upperclassmen, too," Faisal says. "Not saying they'll participate, but if we could get almost everyone, maybe it could work."

"It's gone on too long," a tenth year says. "My best friend got kicked out last year. We have to say enough's enough."

We decide on the date. Thursday. Three days away. Enough time to let people know. Enough time to organize. We settle on third period. Right before lunch.

"Let's meet out back, by the soccer field," Faisal says.

"We'll need some protest chants," Humza adds.

"On it," says Marwan. "How about: 'Heck no! they can't go!'"

"Whoa," Naveed says. "That was fast!"

"Got more where that came from." Marwan grins.

I hesitate. "It's great, but you need to know this is a huge risk."

"It's like you said," Humza says. "One person might not make a difference, but all of us? They can't look away."

People start talking over one another. When I look at Naveed, his eyes are moist. I know what he's feeling. I feel it, too: Everyone who is here came because they want to help us stay. We started this year alone. But somewhere along the way, we found a community.

Chapter 40

*O*mar. Come here, we gotta talk to you."

Marwan and Aiden wave me over to their table in art class the next day. Presentations are officially over, and now Mr. Adeel is letting us hang out and make whatever art we want. There are boxes strewn all over filled with newspaper clippings and odds and ends like buttons and leftover construction paper and clipped ribbons. The classroom buzzes with noisy conversations.

"Got some art to show you," Marwan says mischievously when I approach.

He hands me a folded sheet of paper. Opening it, there's an illustration of a raised fist and the words:

What: *Project Justice*

Why: *To stand up for Naveed and Omar!*

When: *Walk out of your classroom Thursday, 11 a.m.*

Where: *Meet at the soccer field*

PASS IT ON

"Wow. But flyers—" I begin. "What if a teacher sees them?"

"We're only making a few," Aiden says. "We'll pass them around in class. Nothing on bulletin boards or anything. This has got to happen as quietly as possible."

"And the other thing." Marwan nods to Aiden.

They flip over the poster boards on their desk. The first one says: *Justice Now*. The second one: *Step Out*.

"What do you think?" Marwan asks nervously. "The *Step Out* one might seem weird, but—"

"We got the idea from your presentation." Aiden clears his throat. "I googled Shehzil Malik, and she had a photo with those words. About protesting. I thought it was pretty on point, since that's literally what we're doing."

I'm speechless.

"That's . . . so great," I manage to say.

"I'm going to see if I can sneak some poster boards," says Marwan. "We can make more after school in the rec room."

A voice interrupts us. "What sort of collaboration do we have here?"

All of us startle. It's Mr. Adeel. Before we can hide the posters, he sees them—and the flyer lying on top.

After reading them, he looks at me.

"I can explain," I say quickly. "This paper, it just—"

"What paper?" Mr. Adeel asks. He rests a hand on my shoulder. "I see some nice art. And some very good friends."

Chapter 41

It's Wednesday night. Technically Thursday. Midnight has come and gone. My body is tired, but I can't sleep. I saw Faisal and the others by the mural today. They were working on it for hours. Sketching something I couldn't make out. I'd normally have joined them, but today passed by in a blur. Even now, this late into the night, I'm a jumble of nerves. My entire body is on edge. Tomorrow's the day. Will it work?

"You up?" I whisper.

"Yep," Kareem replies. "Can't sleep either."

"Marwan and Humza said lots of people are planning to participate. But I don't know . . . It's one thing to think it's a cool idea when you're with your friends and making posters, but each person is going to have to decide for themselves if they're going to participate. If they change their minds, then what? We need more options."

"Aiden's talking to his dad," Kareem says. "Marwan and Humza said they talked to their parents, too. But—"

"Not holding my breath," I say.

"Omar." Kareem pauses. Despite the darkness, I can see his somber expression as he studies the ceiling. "My dad found a flyer on the ground."

I sit up.

"Is he going to say something?"

"No, no." Kareem shakes his head. "He wouldn't do that . . . But he told me not to take part."

"Oh." A rush of relief sweeps through me. "Of course not! You can't be part of this."

"I wanted to." Kareem's voice wavers. "I told him we *all* have to put our foot down or the message won't be as strong. But he said I can't take that kind of a risk. He was so scared. I've never seen him like that."

"As much as it will hurt to get kicked out, I'd feel a million times worse if you got your scholarship revoked because of me. Your father's right. You can't walk out."

"We really need everyone else to step out tomorrow, then," Kareem says quietly.

We lie in our beds in silence. The clock ticks in the distance. He's right. We really do need everyone. Not only for Naveed and me, but for those who will come after us.

Still, walking out is a lot to ask of people. And there is no plan B.

Chapter 42

I can't touch it. I can't taste it. I can't even see it. But I feel it: There is a crackling energy in the air.

As I sit through biology and math, my body feels like it's buzzing.

I know everything is going at the same pace it always does, but it's all moving at a crawl today. Maybe it's because I barely slept all night, but I'm noticing every little thing. The furtive glance Humza sends in my direction. How Naveed can't stop biting his nails. Aiden constantly checking the clock.

And now it's here. History. Third period. The last class before lunch. And at eleven o'clock on the dot, if everyone does what they said they would, we'll get up and walk out.

I watch the clock ticking slowly. Too slowly. Will people do it? Will they actually risk getting into serious trouble for Naveed and me? The thought of getting up and walking out in the middle of class makes my own palms feel clammy.

The minute hand ticks past the quarter mark. To the half mark. And then it inches to eleven.

There's a click.

It's time.

Some kids check their watches. A few peek at the wall clock. But no one's moved.

My stomach twists. Did the plan get called off? Or did everyone change their minds?

Marwan looks at me. He clears his throat. He stands up.

Humza, too. Next is Aiden. Then Jibril.

The teacher's still turned away from us when all the boys in the last row push back their chairs.

When Mr. Khalid turns around, he frowns.

"What is this?" he asks.

Naveed bites his lip. Worry is written all over his face. But when our eyes meet, he nods. Pushing my chair back, I rise. The petition is in my hands; I clutch it tight. Naveed stands up, too.

"What's going on?" Mr. Khalid asks again. "Class is still in session. Let's take our seats."

Over his protests, we step out of the classroom.

It's happening. It happened.

Everyone in my class walked out.

Other classroom doors fling open. Students pour out. We all march toward the back of the building. I get caught up in the stream of people. There aren't twenty or thirty of us here. At least one hundred of us are walking down the hallway right now.

Someone slides into lockstep with me. I falter when I see who it is.

"Kareem." I pause. "No. You can't."

"I have to," he says.

His father's eyes widen as we walk past him. I see his fear. But glancing at Kareem, I know he won't change his mind.

We all step onto the grassy soccer field. It's already filled with people. My fellow schoolmates. All here for us.

"Equality for us! Equality for all!" shouts Marwan.

Without missing a beat, everyone chants along.

Teachers and staff who work at Ghalib—Mr. Adeel, Mr. Nawaz, even Shuaib and Basem—hurry outside and stare at the scene unfolding.

"No way! Let them stay!"

The chants get louder. I shout alongside the others until my throat grows hoarse.

Then I notice Faisal. He's with a bunch of other upper-classmen at the mural wall. They're painting.

As the chants continue, I walk closer to the wall. The mural is fully sketched out in charcoal. There's a sun with rays extended outward and a wall of students—rows and rows of them with their arms outstretched toward a group of boys floating away like balloons. Each drifting kid's ankle is caught by the hands of someone on the ground. The ones on safe ground are not letting them go: *Ghalib Academy—all for one and one for all.*

I glance at Faisal, and he smiles at me. I pick up a paintbrush and join the other boys painting in the sun. When I dip my brush into the yellow paint, I see him: Headmaster Moiz. He's at the top of the steps. His hands in his pockets. He watches all of us, and then his attention settles on me. I clutch the paintbrush in my hands.

I start painting and don't stop.

Chapter 43

Headmaster Moiz sits behind his desk when I enter his office. The air feels charged and tense. I should feel afraid, but instead it's like I'm made of air. I can't stop replaying what happened. Practically an entire school stood up at the exact same time. They chanted and protested. For me. For Naveed. And for all the others who had to leave too soon. It almost seems like a dream, but it happened. It really happened.

Before he can say a word, I slide the petition toward him.

"Please," I say. "Please read this first."

I try my best to stay still as he reads my message. He flips through the signatures and then places it down on the table.

"Your grammar has improved," he says. "It's a well-written petition."

I blink at the unexpected response.

"This was a first," he says. "Not the first petition, of course. But a walkout? I must admit, it was impressive."

Impressive? I expected him to yell at me. To tell me to collect my things and exit at once. But he doesn't seem angry. Seconds pass in silence.

"Do you know who you remind me of?" he finally says. "Me."

"*What?*" I stare at him.

"I know." He smiles a little. "Hard to believe. But it's true. I see in you a lot of who I was . . . or perhaps more accurately, who I wish I had been. I've told you I am a Ghalib Academy graduate myself. Thirty-five years to the day." He pauses. "I was in the first class of Scholars."

I take in his dark glasses, his fancy suit, his firm disposition.

"How . . . ?" My mind races with questions. *Headmaster Moiz was a Scholar?* This makes no sense.

"We began as a scholarship class of twenty that year. Only three of us went on to graduate. I found it unfair then. Still do."

"I thought you were weeding us out."

"Weeding out?" He pauses. "Suppose I can't blame anyone for thinking that. The scholarship requirements were established well before my time. I hoped by providing a small group setting it might help improve your grades. It's what all the literature says anyhow. But I guess I've gotten rusty as a teacher."

"It worked," I say quickly. "I'm getting excellent grades in all my subjects now. But it takes time to learn the system. You're kicking us out before we got a real chance."

"Unfortunately, despite all appearances, I do not have the final say on such matters. I answer to a board."

"But couldn't you at least talk to the board? They trust you enough to lead this school. They'd listen to you."

He looks at me. I hold his gaze. There was a time when his somber expression would send my pulse racing, but it's because I'd assumed a lot about him. Just as much as I thought he'd assumed of me. The silence between us grows as the seconds pass. He looks down at the petition. He flips to the last page. He lifts his pen and signs it.

"I will speak to the board," he says. "I will share your petition. We meet on the first Friday after school is out. I will let you know what they say."

Chapter 44

I pull my suitcase from the closet. Kareem's on his bed, his back against the wall. Aiden sits cross-legged next to him. None of us speak. What is there to say?

It takes hardly any time to pack up my things. I pull my photo of my mother and me from the dresser, fold up the poster, take out my clothing from the drawers. Naveed knocks on the door and steps inside. His suitcase is smaller than mine, bulging at the edges. His book bag is slung over his shoulder. A whole school year is over, and we are going home.

"I can't believe it didn't work," Aiden says.

"We don't know yet. They're thinking about it," Naveed says. "So . . . maybe."

"Yeah," Kareem says. "Maybe."

"It's weird, but I feel lighter," Naveed says. "It's like I've been wondering for so long if the hammer will drop. Waiting for it was almost worse than it happening. But we did everything we could. We said our piece, you know? No matter what happens. At least we have that."

We *did* give it everything we could. But I think of all we missed: the movie nights, the soccer games, the evening hangouts in the rec room. We missed out on so many things. And for what? We're leaving anyway.

Still, I'm glad to see Naveed looking at peace. Maybe I'll get there, too, in time.

"My dad finally called Moiz. This morning," Aiden says. "He left a voice message for him. Once I have an update, I'll let you know."

"We're not going to give up," Kareem says. "No way."

I understand why they want to keep hoping, but as optimistic as I want to feel, I'm tired.

My phone rings. Malik Uncle. He's in the parking lot waiting to take me home.

"I'll call you over the break," Kareem says. "And hey . . . you'll both be back. I know it."

"We'll keep in touch," Aiden says.

But will we really? Something heavy lodges in my throat. I understand now why Aiden found it hard to get too close to people, only to have to say goodbye. And there are no other people I've grown as close to as the ones in this room. This school was our universe. We shared the same orbit here. And even if we do manage to stay in touch, it'll never be the same again.

. . .

I shield my eyes from the bright sun when I step onto the school's front lawn. The front door flies open again. When I look up, Mr. Adeel and Shuaib are striding toward me.

"Now, I *know* you weren't planning to sneak out without saying goodbye, were you?" Shuaib says.

"Oh, I'm not—" I'm about to protest. Except I kind of was. I'm not sure how to say goodbye to them. They were my safe space in this school. Knowing I probably won't ever see them again . . . it hurts a whole lot.

"The walkout was incredible," Mr. Adeel says. "You really pulled it off. Never saw a thing like it in all my years. And the mural. Nice statement."

"Don't know if it'll do anything," I reply.

"For what it's worth," he continues, "I spoke to Headmaster Moiz this morning. Staff and teachers signed your petition. You're not on your own. We're going to keep on pushing on our end."

Shuaib pats my back. "And whatever happens, don't forget there's more out there than Ghalib. The world is wide open for you, Omar. You've only just begun. Don't let anyone tell you otherwise. Who knows? Maybe you'll become the best chef this country's ever seen. I'd put money on that. I know genius when I see it."

"Or maybe you'll be Pakistan's premier collage artist?" Mr. Adeel interjects with a wink. "You've got quite a knack for that, too!"

"Thanks for believing in me." I give them each a hug. "It's good to know you think I've got some skills to fall back on."

"You hold tight to your stubborn optimism," Mr. Adeel says.

"I'll try."

But the truth is, right now, it feels like a lot less work to let go.

• • •

Malik Uncle waves as I approach.

"Look at you!" he exclaims. "You're almost as tall as me now. Can't wait to hear about your semester when we get home."

I climb aboard as he revs up his engine. And then we're off, flying through the dusty streets. Each forward motion getting us closer to my village. To home.

As the wind whips against my face, reality finally sinks in. I'm going home. And I probably won't be returning. Tears fall down my cheeks. I'll have to tell my mother. Amal. My village. I didn't just fail myself. I failed everyone.

Chapter 45

My mother's waiting by the front steps of Amal's house when we pull up. I run straight into her arms, and she hugs me tight.

"Omar!" Amal hurries out of the house. "Welcome home!"

"Come on in," Amal's mother says. She ushers me toward their home. "We made dinner. All your favorites. Let's eat before it gets cold."

Numbly, I follow them. Everyone settles down to eat.

My mother reaches out and touches my arm. "I can hardly believe you're back for the whole summer!"

My lower lip trembles.

"Omar," she says urgently. "What's wrong?"

"There's something I need to tell all of you."

They listen as I share everything. I leave nothing out. About the scholarship requirements and my grades. The tutoring and late nights. The chores. I tell them about the petition and the walkout. The protest and the mural. The chants.

And I fill them in about my conversation with Headmaster Moiz.

My mother's eyes well with tears.

"I ruined everything," I whisper. "I'm sorry, Amma. I never meant to disappoint you."

"Disappointed? In *you*?" She grips my hand in hers. "These aren't tears of disappointment. How could I ever be disappointed after all you've done? I'm heartbroken to know how much you suffered. Why didn't you tell me, Omar?"

"I didn't want to worry you."

"This was a lot to bear. You didn't have to deal with it all alone," Malik Uncle says.

"I wasn't alone," I tell them. "I had friends. And the whole school tried in the end."

"It still might work, right?" Amal says. "He said he'd talk to the board."

"I'm not getting my hopes up."

"Well, even if Ghalib Academy says you can't go back, so what," says Amal. "You'll find a way."

"What way is that?"

"I don't know," Amal says. "But there'll be something else. Ghalib isn't the only school out there."

"Which will have application fees and other requirements."

"And we'll help with that," Uncle says. "We'll make it work."

"They're right, Omar. We'll figure something out," my mother says. Her eyes are still moist, but she's smiling. How can she smile after hearing this news?

I think about the ghost boys. They might haunt my dreams, but they aren't actually ghosts. Just because they left the school doesn't mean they stopped existing. They're out there. And Shuaib had mentioned one of the kids figured out a way forward. They didn't stop trying after they left Ghalib. Not if they were the kind of kids to work so hard to get into Ghalib in the first place.

Maybe I'd been focusing on the wrong thing this whole time. Instead of being stubbornly optimistic about sticking around at Ghalib Academy, I should have been stubbornly optimistic about believing in myself.

Looking at everyone around me, I see that they do.

Chapter 46

Three weeks. That's how long I've been home.

Every morning, I eat breakfast with my mother and Amal's family. I run errands at the market. I pray Maghrib most evenings at the masjid next to the literacy center. I've already had not one but *two* book-club meetings with Amal. Most evenings, once the sun is less painfully hot, I play soccer with my friends near the sugarcane fields. Fuad *still* swears he'll quit playing with us at the end of each game, making us all laugh.

It's good to be home. Like Naveed, I'm starting to feel lighter. It's nice not having the constant worry to perform hanging over my head anymore. I get to just *be*. I almost forgot what that felt like. I'm happy to hang out with my friends and my mother, and most days it honestly feels like I never even left.

But then there are other times when I can't help but think about Ghalib. In a few weeks everyone returns. Except me. The Friday board meeting Headmaster Moiz told me about came and went. I never heard back.

This morning I visited the local secondary school with my mother. It's two stories with a courtyard and picnic benches. A fenced lawn out back for sports. There are no sleek computer labs, and I doubt there'll be archery or science clubs, but Fuad and Zaki go there, so I'll have built-in friends. And they like it.

I think of Shuaib and how his dreams changed. This school won't be Ghalib, but it's still an education. There'll be plenty of soccer to play, and who knows, maybe I'll start an astronomy club of my own there. And at least there we won't be treated like we're a thorn in someone's side.

When the phone in my pocket rings, my heart leaps. But looking at the number, I see it's not the school.

"Hey, Kareem," I answer.

"Any word?" he asks.

"Nothing yet."

"Oh." I can hear his disappointment before he turns cheery. "Well. It could still happen. They didn't say no yet."

He's home for the summer and tells me about his daily trips to Danawala's candy stand. Splashing in the swimming hole with his cousins. Sleeping on his old charpay under the stars. In the background I can hear the laughter of a little kid. His sister. It'd been a long year for Kareem. I'm glad he's home.

"Call me as soon as you know?" he asks.

"You'll be the first call I make," I promise.

When we hang up, surprisingly, I feel okay. We did everything we could have, and whether or not it's in my destiny to continue at Ghalib, I have no regrets.

· · ·

I'm setting a bowl of milk out for the cats later that day when I hear a shriek. I straighten. It came from Amal's home. I break into a run through the courtyard, yank open the back door, and practically skid inside. Amal's by the door. Her sisters and parents, too. They're all smiling.

"I can't believe it," Amal says breathlessly. She's holding a letter. Her hands are shaking.

"Is that *the* letter?" I ask.

"Yes! I got in to Iqra! Can you believe it? Now I have to figure out—" Her voice drops off. She winces. "Oh, Omar . . . I'm sorry."

"Sorry for what? This is the best news anyone could hope for!"

Her mother takes the letter from her to read. Uncle pulls Amal into a tight embrace. Within moments everyone's hugging her. I watch from the sofa. I had no doubt Amal would get in! And knowing Amal, she'll set the grading curve for the entire school.

• • •

I'm sitting on my charpay and reading a book a little later when I hear a light knock three times against our door.

Amal's signal.

I'd seen her earlier, but we hadn't had a chance to actually talk. Slipping on my shoes, I make my way through the swaying sugarcane fields until the stream is in sight.

Amal sits on the fallen tree, studying her lap. I hurry toward her, but as I grow closer, my pace slows. The letter on her lap is not her acceptance letter. The blue-and-yellow eagle insignia of Ghalib Academy is stamped on the front.

"Fozia Auntie dropped it by just now," she says. "Got delivered to her by accident."

"What . . . what does it say?"

"I didn't open it. But I wanted to be here when you did. In case you needed to talk."

In case they say I can't return. Amal looks at me. She smiles, but I see the worry in her eyes.

I take the envelope from her. I stare at the embossed seal. When I was accepted to Ghalib, the headmaster had called me himself to tell me the news. A letter can't be good. I take a deep breath. No matter what this letter says, it does not contain my fate. If Ghalib is a solid no, my future isn't over.

Gingerly, I open the envelope. I pull out the folded paper. I read the words. Then I read them again.

Omar Ali,

The board has reviewed your petition for an amendment to the rules governing scholarship students and, after careful consideration, has resolved to amend the grade-point-average standards for scholarship students. They will now be aligned with those of the rest of the student body. We will also be instituting a probationary period for those who fall below so they can receive extra guidance and counseling.

This notice reverses your dismissal. We are pleased to welcome your return as a student at Ghalib Academy.

Sincerely,

Ghalib Board of Trustees

My hands shake. I read the letter again. And then a third time, just to be sure. I did it. We—all of us at Ghalib—did it. We changed the unchangeable rule, not only for ourselves but for everyone who'll come after us.

"Well? Tell me! What does it say?" Amal exclaims.

"I'm—I'm going back."

"Omar!" She leaps up and hugs me. "I knew it. I knew it!"

We both start laughing, and when we stop, I look out at the swaying sugarcanes. The stream trickling at its ever-steady pace behind us. The clouds that pass overhead. This always gives me comfort and always will. So much has changed. But I'm the same Omar.

What we fought for at Ghalib is really happening. Kids like us will get to breathe a little easier. There'll be more to work on so we're not treated like second-class citizens, but this is a good start. And right now? I'm happy knowing that this fall I'll be joining the soccer team. Signing up for astronomy club. I will see my friends again.

But more than that, bigger than that, I know that no matter what galaxy I get spun into, I will rise to face the challenge. I will be okay.

Acknowledgments

Every book takes a village, and I'm eternally grateful for my community. First and foremost, thank you, Nancy Paulsen, for believing in my stories and being a safe space to share the draftiest of first drafts. I am grateful for our creative partnership and friendship.

Thank you to Sara LaFleur, Cindy Howle, Carmela Iaria, Venessa Carson, Trevor Ingerson, Summer Ogata, Rachel Wease, Lindsey Andrews, Deborah Kaplan, and the entire team at Penguin Young Readers. I am lucky to be part of the Penguin family.

Thank you to Taylor Martindale Kean for your help with this book. Thank you also to my agent, Faye Bender.

My gratitude to the brilliant Shehzil Malik both for being a source of creative inspiration for Omar himself and for once again creating a brilliant cover.

Thank you to Cylinda Parga, Yen M. Tang, Ayesha Mattu, Tracy Lopez, Becky Albertalli, S. K. Ali, Sabaa Tahir, and Samira Ahmed for your friendship. Thank you to Saira Adeel and Adeel Khalid for your advice and feedback along the way. Mr. Adeel encapsulates both of your warm and generous hearts.

Thank you, Ami and Abu, for everything. Omar's mother embodies the unconditional love and support you've given me through all of life's ups and downs.

Thank you to my husband—you helped make writing possible for me during a very difficult year. To my boys: You remain the lights in my life.

And last but not least, thank *you*, dear reader. Thank you for reading my stories, for inviting Amal and now Omar into your homes, libraries, and classrooms. Omar's story is fictional, but I've seen his optimism and his determination in countless children I've worked with as a teacher and met through school visits over the years. His struggle to belong and to overcome seemingly impossible circumstances is something many can relate to. If you are reading these words, I hope that no matter how tough things might get, you always and forever remain stubbornly optimistic, like Omar.